Love and Freindship

Jane Austen was born in Hampshire in 1775. The daughter of a country rector, without advantages of education or travel, she wrote novels which established her as one of the great writers of any age. These include *Sense and Sensibility, Pride and Prejudice, Emma* and *Northanger Abbey.* Jane Austen did not marry and died in 1817.

In 1869, from the Vicarage at Bray, her nephew wrote in his memoir of Jane Austen, "There was in her nothing eccentric or angular; no ruggedness of temper; no singularity of manner; none of the morbid sensibility of exaggeration of feeling, which not unfrequently accompanies great talents... Hers was a mind well balanced on a basis of good sense, sweetened by an affectionate heart, and regulated by fixed principles; so that she was to be distinguished from many other amiable and sensible women only by that peculiar genius which shines out in her works."

JANE AUSTEN

Love and Freindship

AND
OTHER EARLY WORKS

including

THE THREE SISTERS
LESLEY CASTLE
A COLLECTION OF LETTERS
A HISTORY OF ENGLAND

Illustrated by Suzanne Perkins
Introduction by Geraldine Killalea

Harmony Books/New York

This edition published in 1981 by Harmony Books, a division of Crown Publishers, Inc., One Park Avenue, New York, New York 10016.

Published in Great Britain in 1978 by The Women's Press Limited, A Member of the Namara Group, 12 Ellesmere Road, Bow, London E3 5QX.

Printed in the United States of America.

Library of Congress Cataloging in Publication Data

Austen, Jane, 1775-1817.
  Love and freindship [sic] and other early works.

  CONTENTS: Love and freindship.—Lesley Castle.—
The history of England.—[etc.]
  I. Title.
PR4034.L6   1981   823'.7   80-25524
ISBN: 0-517-544598 (cloth)
      0-517-543729 (paper)

10 9 8 7 6 5 4 3 2 1

First Edition

CONTENTS

INTRODUCTION

This volume contains a selection from Jane Austen's earliest writings, the Juvenilia, not published during her lifetime and only rarely since. These youthful works of a brilliant writer and perceptive woman display aspects of her talent which do not appear elsewhere, and which while directly relevant to the background of eighteenth-century fiction she mocks, are still apposite in the twentieth century. Their maturity is astonishing, their irony enlightening, and their gaiety contagious.

The date on the manuscript of "Love and Freindship" ("Finis June 13th 1790") reveals Jane Austen's precocious literary skill. She was then less than fifteen. One is tempted to draw parallels with Daisy Ashford's *The Young Visiters* written by another precocious and perceptive child. However, the differences are greater than those between a nine-year-old Victorian and a fourteen-year-old country rector's daughter a hundred years earlier. Daisy Ashford's is the charming work of a most unusual child; Jane Austen's writing reveals a critical awareness of current literary fashion and is in fact directed towards debunking the follies of contemporary novels rather than recording the contemporary social scene. Her swooning heroines do not reflect a real world littered with prostrate women; rather, they reflect a world in which the styles and mores of fiction had become wholly artificial and stultifying. By the end of the eighteenth century the actions of characters in sentimental novels obeyed the "laws" of fiction rather than probability, and the author's point of view was all too often determined by literary habit. The notion of "sensibility" had degenerated from "moral sense" to "feeling", or perhaps more accurately, the ability to display emotion. Physiological display of emotion through trembling, tears, changing colour, hysteria, fainting or madness, that is, sentimental performance, was directly related to sincerity or even personal worth and, indeed, regarded as a reflection of personal value.

This absurd convention led to a well-established tradition of burlesque. It is to this tradition that "Love and Freindship" belongs. It is a perfect parody. The breathlessly evolving plot defies summary. It is a gorgeous sequence of all the stock situations and stock responses of the novel of sensibility: exotic parentage, unexpected encounters, love at first sight, impetuous marriages, revolt against authority, flights out of danger, dramatic recognition scenes. Yet, throughout, we are made aware of the *normal* as well as the conventional *literary* reaction to such situations, and it is the contrast between the laws of fiction and the standards of probable social behaviour which exposes the essential unreality of eighteenth-century popular novels. The dishonest emotion on which the novel of sensibility is founded engenders dishonesty of action: Edward "gracefully" purloins a considerable sum of money from his unworthy father's escritoire; discussing a generous benefactor, Sophia and Laura agree that "it would be a proper treatment of so vile a wretch as MacDonald to deprive him of money". When display of emotion is the only measure of value, all other standards are jettisoned. False sensibility is finally founded upon self-interest.

What distinguishes Jane Austen's brilliant burlesque from the novels of sensibility she attacks is not her exaggeration but her exposure of the selfish foundation of sensibility. One of the conventions parodied in "Love and Freindship" is the equation of fainting with delicate sensibility. Sophia and Laura collapse at every crisis; their characteristic response is, "Ah! What could we do but what we did! We sighed and fainted on the sofa." Sophia's last words to Laura again emphasise this egotism: "Beware of swoons Dear Laura ... A frenzy fit is not one quarter so pernicious; it is an exercise to the Body and if not too violent, is I dare say conducive to Health in its consequences — Run mad as often as you chuse; but do not faint —"

How did a girl as young as Jane Austen acquire the perspective necessary to penetrate the sham of contemporary fiction, and the skill to parody it so effectively? At least part of the answer may stem from the literary ambience of the Austen household, where critical discussion of current fiction was common. We know also that at about this time Jane's brothers James and Henry produced a periodical called "The Loiterer" in which there were a number of essays on literary style and convention. It is likely that Jane originally wrote for circulation only within the family, and probably for reading aloud. In the first, posthumous, edition of *Northanger Abbey* and *Persuasion* (1818), Henry Austen recalls that his sister's works "were never heard to so much advantage as from her own mouth; for she partook largely in all the best gifts of the comic muse".

When she revised her notebooks later in her life she amended the spelling of "Love and Freindship" to "Love and Friendship" and made some improvements to the text. In this edition those improvements are generally followed, but the original oddities and inconsistencies of spelling have been deliberately retained to convey the endearing charm of her youthful manuscript.

The "History of England", the second work in this volume, is dated 26 November 1791. The letters in "Lesley Castle" are dated 3 January to 13 April 1792, a period probably close to their actual composition. "A Collection of Letters" is dedicated to Miss Cooper, a childhood friend who married Thomas Williams on 11 December 1792. These pieces, and "Love and Freindship", all come from *Volume the Second* of the three notebooks of her Juvenilia. "The three Sisters" is taken from *Volume the First* which, though undated, is believed to have been written before 1792. Thus all the pieces in this edition were completed before Jane turned seventeen. Her technical skills were to grow, but these early works show already an uncannily apt combination of comic inventiveness and naturalism as well as the vividness and accuracy of her later dialogue.

The letter as a story-telling device was common in eighteenth-century fiction, though not used in Jane Austen's mature work. In "The three Sisters"—a marvellous example of Jane Austen's gift for subversive irony—the letter convention is used to compare two sets of attitudes to marriage, and in particular its social and economic implications. Mary Stanhope's first two letters reveal her as shallow, jealous and avaricious. Her sister Georgiana continues the narrative, describing Mary's behaviour with ironic perception. We see here also Jane Austen's understanding of marriage as defining a woman's life, not through choice necessarily, but through economic necessity. This awareness gives Jane Austen a place among the earliest feminists.

A feminist view is also apparent in Jane Austen's depiction

of Miss Charlotte Lutterell in "Lesley Castle", a fully-realised woman of independent mind as well as a paragon of housewifely virtues. Almost alone among Jane Austen's heroines (the other being Emma) she does not define herself in relation to men, and has no aspirations to marriage as a means of economic or social survival. She has her own unique sense of moral values and a clear and consistent self image.

Jane Austen did not confuse substance with form. Indeed, a most compelling aspect of her work is the revelation of moral value implicit in ordinary social behaviour. One wonders how this woman who deplored excessive sensibility would have regarded some of the more excessive manifestations of contemporary society. Her argument against confusing display of feeling with moral judgment is still a relevant one, and we do well to apply her astringent penetration to our own times.

GERALDINE KILLALEA

LOVE
&
FREINDSHIP

A NOVEL IN A SERIES OF LETTERS.
"Deceived in Freindship & Betrayed in Love"

Letter the First From Isabel to Laura

How often, in answer to my repeated intreaties that you would give my Daughter a regular detail of the Misfortunes and Adventures of your Life, have you said "No, my freind never will I comply with your request till I may no longer in Danger of again experiencing such dreadful ones." Surely that time is now at hand. You are this Day 55. If a woman may ever be said to be in safety from the determined Perseverance of disagreable Lovers and the cruel Persecutions of obstinate Fathers, surely it must be at such a time of Life.

Isabel.

Letter 2d   Laura to Isabel

Altho' I cannot agree with you in supposing that I shall never again be exposed to Misfortunes as unmerited as those I have already experienced, yet to avoid the imputation of Obstinacy or ill-nature, I will gratify the curiosity of your daughter; and may the fortitude with which I have suffered the many Afflictions of my past Life, prove to her a useful Lesson for the support of those which may befall her in her own.

Laura

Letter 3d   Laura to Marianne

As the Daughter of my most intimate freind I think you entitled to that knowledge of my unhappy Story, which your Mother has so often solicited me to give you.

My Father was a native of Ireland & an inhabitant of Wales; My Mother was the natural Daughter of a Scotch Peer by an italian Opera-girl—I was born in Spain & received my Education at a Convent in France.

When I had reached my eighteenth Year I was re-
called by my Parents to my paternal roof in Wales. Our
mansion was situated in one of the most romantic parts
of the Vale of Uske. Tho' my Charms are now considerably softened and somewhat impaired by the Misfortunes
I have undergone, I was once beautiful. But lovely as I
was the Graces of my Person were the least of my Perfections. Of every accomplishment accustomary to my
sex, I was Mistress. When in the Convent, my progress
had always exceeded my instructions, my Acquirements
had been wonderfull for my Age, and I had shortly sur-
passed my Masters.

In my Mind, every Virtue that could adorn it was
centered; it was the Rendezvous of every good Quality &
of every noble sentiment.

A sensibility too tremblingly alive to every affliction of
my Freinds, my Acquaintance and particularly to every
affliction of my own, was my only fault, if a fault it could
be called. Alas! how altered now! Tho' indeed my own
misfortunes do not make less impression on me than they
ever did, yet now I never feel for those of an other. My
accomplishments too, begin to fade—I can neither sing
so well nor Dance so gracefully as I once did—and I have
entirely forgot the *Minuet Dela Cour*.

Adeiu.

Laura

Letter 4th   Laura to Marianne

Our neighbourhood was small, for it consisted only of
your mother. She may probably have already told you
that being left by her Parents in indigent Circumstances
she had retired into Wales on eoconomical motives.
There is was, our freindship first commenced. Isabel was
then one and twenty—Tho' pleasing both in her Person
and Manners (between ourselves) she never possessed the
hundredth part of my Beauty or Accomplishments.

Isabel had seen the World. She had passed 2 Years at one of the first Boarding schools in London; had spent a fortnight in Bath & had supped one night in Southampton.

"Beware my Laura (she would often say) Beware of the insipid Vanities and idle Dissipations of the Metropolis of England; Beware of the unmeaning Luxuries of Bath & of the Stinking fish of Southampton."

"Alas! (exclaimed I) how am I to avoid those evils I shall never be exposed to? What probability is there of my ever tasting the Dissipations of London, the Luxuries of Bath or the stinking Fish of Southampton? I who am doomed to waste my Days of Youth & Beauty in an humble Cottage in the Vale of Uske."

Ah! little did I then think I was ordained so soon to quit that humble Cottage for the Deceitfull Pleasures of the World.

adeiu
Laura

Letter 5th   Laura to Marianne

One Evening in December as my Father, my Mother and myself, were arranged in social converse round our Fireside, we were on a sudden, greatly astonished, by hearing a violent knocking on the outward Door of our rustic Cot.

My Father started—"What noise is that," (said he.) "It sounds like a loud rapping at the Door"—(replied my Mother.) "it does indeed." (cried I.) "I am of your opinion; (said my Father) it certainly does appear to proceed from some uncommon violence exerted against our unoffending Door." "Yes (exclaimed I) I cannot help thinking it must be somebody who knocks for Admittance."

"That is another point (replied he;) We must not pretend to determine on what motive the person may knock

—tho' that someone *does* rap at the Door, I am partly convinced."

Here, a 2d tremendous rap interrupted my Father in his speech and somewhat alarmed my Mother and me.

"Had we not better go and see who it is,? (said she) the Servants are out." "I think we had." (replied I.) "Certainly, (added my Father) by all means." "Shall we go now?" (said my Mother.) "The sooner the better." (answered he). "Oh! let no time be lost." (cried I.)

A third more violent Rap than ever again assaulted our ears. "I am certain there is somebody knocking at the Door." (said my Mother.) "I think there must," (replied my Father) "I fancy the Servants are returned; (said I) I think I hear Mary going to the Door." "I'm glad of it (cried my Father) for I long to know who it is."

I was right in my Conjecture; for Mary instantly entering the Room, informed us that a young Gentleman & his Servant were at the Door, who had lossed their way, were very cold and begged leave to warm themselves by our fire.

"Wont you admit them?" (said I) "You have no objection, my Dear?" (said my Father.) "None in the World." (replied my Mother.)

Mary, without waiting for any further commands immediately left the room and quickly returned introducing the most beauteous and amiable Youth, I had ever beheld. The servant, She kept to herself.

My natural Sensibility had already been greatly affected by the sufferings of the unfortunate Stranger and no sooner did I first behold him, than I felt that on him the happiness or Misery of my future Life must depend.

adeiu.

Laura

Letter 6th   Laura to Marianne

The noble Youth informed us that his name was Lindsay —for particular reasons however I shall conceal it under that of Talbot. He told us that he was the son of an English Baronet, that his Mother had been many years no more and that he had a Sister of the middle size. "My Father (he continued) is a mean and mercenary wretch —it is only to such particular freinds as this Dear Party that I would thus betray his failings. Your Virtues my amiable Polydore (addressing himself to my father) yours Dear Claudia and yours my Charming Laura call on me to repose in you, my Confidence." We bowed. "My Father, seduced by the false glare of Fortune and the Deluding Pomp of Title, insisted on my giving my hand to Lady Dorothea. No never exclaimed I. Lady Dorothea is lovely and Engaging; I prefer no woman to her; but know Sir, that I scorn to marry her in compliance with your wishes. No! Never shall it be said that I obliged my Father,"

We all admired the noble Manliness of his reply. He continued.

"Sir Edward was surprized; he had perhaps little expected to meet with so spirited an opposition to his will. 'Where Edward in the name of wonder (said he) did you pick up this unmeaning Gibberish? You have been studying Novels I suspect.' I scorned to answer: it would have been beneath my Dignity. I mounted my Horse and followed by my faithful William set forwards for my Aunts."

"My Father's house is situated in Bedfordshire, my Aunt's in Middlesex, and tho' I flatter myself with being a tolerable proficienz in Geography, I know not how it happened, but I found myself entering this beautifull Vale which I find is in South Wales, when I had expected to have reached my Aunts."

"After having wandered some time on the Banks of the Uske without knowing which way to go, I began to lament my cruel Destiny in the bitterest and most pathetic Manner. It was now perfectly dark, not a single Star was there to direct my steps, and I know not what might have befallen me had I not at length discerned thro' the solemn Gloom that surrounded me a distant Light, which as I approached it, I discovered to be the chearfull Blaze of your fire. Impelled by the combination of Misfortunes under which I laboured, namely Fear, Cold and Hunger I hesitated not to ask admittance which at length I have gained; and now my Adorable Laura (continued he taking my Hand) when may I hope to receive that reward of all the painfull sufferings I have undergone during the course of my Attachment to you, to which I have ever aspired? Oh! when will you reward me with Yourself?"

"This instant, Dear and Amiable Edward." (replied I.). We were immediately united by my Father, who tho' he had never taken orders had been bred to the Church.

adeiu

Laura.

Letter 7th   Laura to Marianne

We remained but a few Days after our Marriage, in the Vale of Uske. After taking an affecting Farewell of my father, my Mother and my Isabel, I accompanied Edward to his Aunt's in Middlesex. Philippa received us both with every expression of affectionate Love. My arrival was indeed a most agreable surprize to her as she had not only been totally ignorant of my Marriage with her Nephew, but had never even had the slightest idea of there being such a person in the World.

Augusta, the sister of Edward was on a visit to her when we arrived. I found her exactly what her Brother had described her to be—of the middle size. She received me with equal surprize though not with equal Cordiality, as Philippa. There was a Disagreable Coldness and Forbidding Reserve in her reception of me which was equally Distressing and Unexpected. None of that interesting Sensibility or amiable Simpathy in her Manners and

Address to me which should have Distinguished our introduction to each other. Her Language was neither warm, nor affectionate, her expressions of regard were neither animated nor cordial; her arms were not opened to receive me to her Heart, tho' my own were extended to press her to mine.

A short Conversation between Augusta and her Brother, which I accidentally overheard encreased my Dislike to her, and convinced me that her Heart was no more formed for the soft ties of Love than for the endearing intercourse of Freindship.

"But do you think that my Father will ever be reconciled to this imprudent connection?" (said Augusta.)

"Augusta (replied the noble Youth) I thought you had a better opinion of me, than to imagine I would so abjectly degrade myself as to consider my Father's Concurrence in any of my Affairs, either of Consequence or concern to me. Tell me Augusta tell me with sincerity; did you ever know me consult his inclinations or follow his Advice in the least trifling Particular since the age of fifteen?"

"Edward (replied she) you are surely too diffident in your own praise. Since you were fifteen only!—My Dear Brother since you were five years old, I entirely acquit you of ever having willingly contributed to the Satisfaction of your Father. But still I am not without apprehensions of your being shortly obliged to degrade yourself in your own eyes by seeking a Support for your Wife in the Generosity of Sir Edward."

"Never, never Augusta will I so demean myself. (said Edward). Support! What Support will Laura want which she can receive from him?"

"Only those very insignificant ones of Victuals and Drink." (answered she.)

"Victuals and Drink! (replied my Husband in almost nobly contemtuous Manner) and dost thou then imagine that there is no other support for an exalted Mind (such

as is my Laura's) than the mean and indelicate employment of Eating and Drinking?"

"None that I know of, so efficacious." (returned
Augusta).

"And did you then never feel the pleasing Pangs of
Love, Augusta? (replied my Edward). Does it appear
impossible to your vile and corrupted Palate, to exist on
Love? Can you not conceive the Luxury of living in
every Distress that Poverty can inflict, with the object of
your tenderest Affection?"

"You are too ridiculous (said Augusta) to argue with;
perhaps however you may in time be convinced that. . ."

Here I was prevented from hearing the remainder of
her Speech, by the Appearance of a very Handsome
Young Woman, who was ushered into the Room at the
Door of which I had been listening. On hearing her announced by the Name of "Lady Dorothea", I instantly
quitted my Post and followed her into the Parlour, for I
well remembered that she was the Lady, proposed as a Wife
for my Edward by the Cruel and Unrelenting Baronet.

Altho' Lady Dorothea's visit was nominally to Philippa
and Augusta, yet I have some reason to imagine that
(acquainted with the Marriage and arrival of Edward)
to see me was a principal motive to it.

I soon perceived that tho' lovely and Elegant in her
Person and tho' Easy and Polite in her Address, she was
of that inferior order of Beings with regard to Delicate
feeling, tender Sentiments, and refined Sensibility, of
which Augusta was one.

She staid but half an hour and neither in the Course
of her Visit, confided to me any of her Secret thoughts,
nor requested me to confide in her, any of mine. You
will easily imagine therefore my Dear Marianne that I
could not feel any ardent Affection or very sincere
Attachment for Lady Dorothea.

Adeiu
Laura

Letter 8th   Laura to Marianne, in continuation

Lady Dorothea had not left us long before another visitor
as unexpected a one as her Ladyship, was announced.
It was Sir Edward, who informed by Augusta of her
Brother's marriage, came doubtless to reproach him for
having dared to unite himself to me without his Knowledge. But Edward foreseeing his Design, approached him
with heroic fortitude as soon as he entered the Room,
and addressed him in the following Manner.

"Sir Edward, I know the motive of your Journey here
—You come with the base Design of reproaching me for
having entered into an indissoluble engagement with my
Laura without your Consent—But Sir, I glory in the
Act—. It is my greatest boast that I have incurred the
Displeasure of my Father!"

So saying, he took my hand and whilst Sir Edward,
Philippa, and Augusta were doubtless reflecting with
Admiration on his undaunted Bravery, led me from the
Parlour to his Father's Carriage, which yet remained at
the Door and in which we were instantly conveyed from
the pursuit of Sir Edward.

The Postilions had at first received orders only to take
the London road; as soon as we had sufficiently reflected
However, we ordered them to Drive to M———. the seat
of Edward's most particular freind, which was but a few
miles distant.

At M———. we arrived in a few hours; and on sending
in our names were immediately admitted to Sophia, the
Wife of Edward's freind. After having been deprived
during the course of 3 weeks of a real freind (for such I
term your Mother) imagine my transports at beholding
one, most truly worthy of the Name. Sophia was rather
above the middle size; most elegantly formed. A soft
Languor spread over her lovely features, but increased
their Beauty.—It was the Charectarestic of her Mind—.
She was all Sensibility and Feeling. We flew into each

L.F.—2

other arms & after having exchanged vows of mutual Freindship for the rest of our Lives, instantly unfolded to each other the most inward Secrets of our Hearts—. We were interrupted in this Delightfull Employment by the entrance of Augustus, (Edward's freind) who was just returned from a solitary ramble.

Never did I see such an affecting Scene as was the meeting of Edward & Augustus.

"My Life! my Soul!" (exlaimed the former) "My Adorable Angel!" (replied the latter) as they flew into each other's arms. It was too pathetic for the feelings of Sophia and myself—We fainted Alternately on a Sofa.

Adeiu
Laura

Letter the 9th   From the Same to the Same

Towards the close of the Day we received the following Letter from Philippa.

"Sir Edward is greatly incensed by your abrupt departure; he has taken back Augusta with him to Bedfordshire. Much as I wish to enjoy again your charming society, I cannot determine to snatch you from that, of such dear & deserving Freinds—When your Visit to them is terminated, I trust you will return to the arms of your"

"Philippa."

We returned a suitable answer to this affectionate Note & after thanking her for her kind invitation assured her that we would certainly avail ourselves of it, whenever we might have no other place to go to. Tho' certainly nothing could to any reasonable Being, have appeared more satisfactory, than so gratefull a reply to her invitation, yet I know not how it was, but she was certainly capricious enough to be displeased with our behaviour and in a few weeks after, either to revenge our Conduct, or releive her own solitude, married a young and illiterate

Fortune-hunter. This imprudent Step (tho' we were sensible that it would probably deprive us of that fortune which Philippa had ever taught us to expect) could not on our own accounts, excite from our exalted Minds a single sigh; yet fearfull lest it might prove a source of endless misery to the deluded Bride, our trembling Sensibility was greatly affected when we were first informed of the Event. The affectionate Entreaties of Augustus and Sophia that we would for ever consider their House as our Home, easily prevailed on us to determine never more to leave them—. In the Society of my Edward & this Amiable Pair, I passed the happiest moments of my Life: Our time was most delightfully spent, in mutual Protestations of Freindship, and in vows of unalterable Love, in which we were secure from being interrupted, by intruding & disagreable Visitors, as Augustus & Sophia had on their first Entrance in the Neighbourhood, taken due care to inform the surrounding Families, that as their Happiness centered wholly in themselves, they wished for no other society. But alas! my Dear Marianne such Happiness as I then enjoyed was too perfect to be lasting. A most severe & unexpected Blow at once destroyed every Sensation of Pleasure. Convinced as you must be from what I have already told you concerning Augustus & Sophia, that there never were a happier Couple, I need not I imagine inform you that their union had been contrary to the inclinations of their Cruel & Mercenary Parents; who had vainly endeavoured with obstinate Perseverance to force them into a Marriage with those whom they had ever abhorred, but with an Heroic Fortitude worthy to be related & Admired, they had both, constantly refused to submit to such despotic Power.

After having so nobly disentangled themselves from the Shackles of Parental Authority, by a Clandestine Marriage, they were determined never to forfeit the good opinion they had gained in the World, in so doing, by accepting any proposals of reconciliation that might be offered them by their Fathers—to this farther tryal of their noble independance however they never were exposed.

They had been married but a few months when our visit to them commenced during which time they had been amply supported by a considerable sum of Money which Augustus had gracefully purloined from his Unworthy father's Escritoire, a few days before his union with Sophia.

By our arrival their Expences were considerably encreased tho' their means for supplying them were then nearly exhausted. But they, Exalted Creatures! scorned to reflect a moment on their pecuniary Distresses & would have blushed at the idea of paying their Debts.— Alas! what was their Reward for such disinterested Behaviour. The beautifull Augustus was arrested and we were all undone. Such perfidious Treachery in the merciless perpetrators of the Deed will shock your gentle nature Dearest Marianne as much as it then affected the Delicate Sensibility of Edward, Sophia, your Laura, & of Augustus himself. To compleat such unparalelled Barbarity we were informed that an Execution in the House would shortly take place. Ah! what could we do but what we did! We sighed & fainted on the Sofa.

Adeiu

Laura

Letter 10th   Laura in continuation

When we were somewhat recovered from the overpowering Effusions of our Grief, Edward desired that we would consider what was the most prudent step to be taken in our unhappy situation while he repaired to his imprisoned freind to lament over his misfortunes. We promised that we would, & he set forwards on his Journey to Town. During his Absence we faithfully complied with

his Desire & after the most mature Deliberation, at
length agreed that the best thing we could do was to
leave the House; of which we every moment expected
the Officers of Justice to take possession. We waited therefore with the greatest impatience, for the return of Edward in order to impart to him the result of our Deliber-
ations—. But no Edward appeared—. In vain did we
count the tedious Moments of his Absence—in vain did we
weep—in vain even did we sigh—no Edward returned—.
This was too cruel, too unexpected a Blow to our Gentle
Sensibility—. we could not support it—we could only
faint—. At length collecting all the Resolution I was
Mistress of, I arose & after packing up some necessary
Apparel for Sophia & myself, I dragged her to a Carriage
I had ordered & instantly we set out for London. As the
Habitation of Augustus was within twelve miles of Town,
it was not long e'er we arrived there, & no sooner had
we entered Holbourn than letting down one of the Front
Glasses I enquired of every decent-looking Person that
we passed "If they had seen my Edward"?

But as we drove too rapidly to allow them to answer
my repeated Enquiries, I gained little, or indeed, no information concerning him. "Where am I to Drive?" said
the Postilion. "To Newgate Gentle Youth (replied I), to
see Augustus." "Oh! no, no, (exclaimed Sophia) I cannot go to Newgate; I shall not be able to support the
sight of my Augustus in so cruel a confinement—my
feelings are sufficiently shocked by the *recital*, of his Distress, but to behold it will overpower my Sensibility." As
I perfectly agreed with her in the Justice of her Sentiments the Postilion was instantly directed to return into
the Country. You may perhaps have been somewhat surprised my Dearest Marianne, that in the Distress I then
endured, destitute of any Support, & unprovided with
any Habitation, I should never once have remembered
my Father & Mother or my paternal Cottage in the Vale
of Uske. To account for this seeming forgetfullness I must

inform you of a trifling Circumstance concerning them
which I have as yet never mentioned—. The death of
my Parents a few weeks after my Departure, is the circumstance I allude to. By their decease I became the
lawfull Inheritress of their House & Fortune. But alas!
the House had never been their own & their Fortune
had only been an Annuity on their own Lives. Such is
the Depravity of the World! To your Mother I should
have returned with Pleasure, should have been happy to
have introduced to her, my Charming Sophia & should
have with Chearfullness have passed the remainder of
my Life in their dear Society in the Vale of Uske, had
not one obstacle to the execution of so agreable a Scheme,
intervened; which was the Marriage & Removal of your
Mother to a Distant part of Ireland.

Adeiu
Laura

Letter 11th   Laura in continuation

"I have a Relation in Scotland (said Sophia to me as
we left London) who I am certain would not hesitate in
receiving me." "Shall I order the Boy to drive there?"
said I—but instantly recollecting myself, exclaimed
"Alas I fear it will be too long a Journey for the Horses."
Unwilling however to act only from my own inadequate
Knowledge of the Strength & Abilities of Horses, I con-
sulted the Postilion, who was entirely of my Opinion
concerning the Affair. We therefore determined to
change Horses at the next Town & to travel Post the
remainder of the Journey.—. When we arrived at the last
Inn we were to stop at, which was but a few miles from
the House of Sophia's Relation, unwilling to intrude
our Society on him unexpected & unthought of, we wrote
a very elegant & well-penned Note to him containing
an Account of our Destitute & melancholy Situation,
and of our intention of spend some months with him in

Scotland. As soon as we had dispatched this letter, we immediately prepared to follow it in person & were stepping into the Carriage for that Purpose when our Attention was attracted by the Entrance of a coroneted Coach & 4 into the Inn-yard. A Gentleman considerably advanced in years, descended from it—. At his first Appearance my Sensibility was wonderfully affected & e'er I had gazed at him a 2d time, an instinctive Sympathy whispered to my Heart, that he was my Grandfather.

Convinced that I could not be mistaken in my conjecture I instantly sprang from the Carriage I had just entered, & following the Venerable Stranger into the Room he had been shewn to, I threw myself on my knees before him & besought him to acknowledge me as his Grand Child.—He started, & after having attentively examined by features, raised me from the Ground & throwing his Grand-fatherly arms around my neck, exclaimed, "Acknowledge thee! Yes dear resemblance of my Laurina & my Laurina's Daughter, sweet image of my Claudia & my Claudia's Mother, I do acknowledge thee as the Daughter of the one & the Grandaughter of the other." While he was thus tenderly embracing me, Sophia astonished at my precipitate Departure, entered the Room in search of me—. No sooner had she caught the eye of the venerable Peer, than he exclaimed with every mark of Astonishment—"Another Grandaughter! Yes, yes, I see you are the Daughter of my Laurina's eldest Girl; Your resembalance to the beauteous Matilda sufficiently proclaims it." "Oh.!" replied Sophia, "when I first beheld you the instinct of Nature whispered me that we were in some degree related—But whether Grandfathers, or Grandmothers, I could not pretend to determine." He folded her in his arms, and whilst they were tenderly embracing, the Door of the Apartment opened and a most beautifull Young Man appeared. On perceiving him Lord St. Clair started and retreating back a few paces, with uplifted Hands, said, "Another Grandchild! What an unexpected Happiness is this! to discover in the space of 3 minutes, as many of my Descendants! This, I am certain is Philander the son of my Laurina's 3d Girl the amiable Bertha; there wants now but the presence of Gustavus to compleat the Union of my Laurina's Grand-Children".

"And here he is; (said a Gracefull Youth who that instant entered the room) here is the Gustavus you desire to see. I am the son of Agatha your Laurina's 4th & Youngest Daughter." "I see you are indeed; replied Lord St. Clair—But tell me (continued he looking fearfully towards the Door) tell me, have I any other Grand-Children in the House." "None my Lord." "Then I will provide for you all without further delay—Here are 4 Banknotes of 50£ each—Take them & remember I have done the Duty of a Grandfather—." He instantly left the Room & immediately afterwards the House.

Adeiu

Laura

Letter the 12th   Laura in continuation

You may imagine how greatly we were surprised by the sudden departure of Lord St. Clair. "Ignoble Grandsire!" exclaimed Sophia. "Unworthy Grandfather!" said I, & instantly fainted in each other's arms. How long we remained in this situation I know not; but when we recovered we found ourselves alone, without either Gustavus, Philander or the Bank-notes. As we were deploring our unhappy fate the Door, of the Apartment opened & "Macdonald" was announced. He was Sophia's cousin. The haste with which he came to our releif so soon after the receipt of our Note, spoke so greatly in his favour that I hesitated not to pronounce him at first sight, a tender & Simpathetic Freind. Alas! he little deserved the name—for though he told us that he was much concerned at our Misfortunes, yet by his own account it appeared that the perusal of them, had neither drawn from him a single sigh, nor induced him to bestow one curse on our vindictive Stars.—. He told Sophia that his Daughter depended on her returning with him to Macdonald-Hall, & that as his Cousin's freind he should be happy to see me there also. To Macdonald-Hall, therefore, we went, and were received with great kindness by Janetta the daughter of Macdonald, & the Mistress of the Mansion. Janetta was then only fifteen; naturally well disposed, endowed with a susceptible Heart, and a simpathetic Disposition, she might, had these amiable Qualities been properly encouraged, have been an ornament to human Nature; but unfortunately her Father possessed not a soul sufficiently exalted to admire so promising a Disposition, and had endeavoured by every means in his power to prevent its encreasing with her Years. He had actually so far extinguished the natural noble Sensibility of her Heart, as to prevail on her to accept an offer from a young man of his Recommendation. They were to be married in a few months, and Graham, was in the House when we arrived. *We* soon saw through his Character.—. He was just such a Man as one might have expected to be the choice of Macdonald. They said he was Sensible, well-informed, and Agreable; we did not pretend to Judge of such trifles, but as we were convinced he had no soul, that he had never read the Sorrows of Werter, & that his Hair bore not the slightest resemblance to Auburn, we were certain that Janetta could feel no affection for him, or at least that she ought to feel none. The very circumstance of his being his father's choice too, was so much in his disfavour, that had he been deserving her, in every other respect yet *that* of itself ought to have been a sufficient reason in the Eyes of Janetta for rejecting him. These considerations we were determined to represent to her in their proper light & doubted not of meeting with the desired success from one naturally so well disposed, whose errors in the Affair had only arisen from a want to proper confidence in her own opinion, & a suitable contempt of her father's. We found her indeed all that our warmest wishes could have hoped for; we had no difficulty to convince her that it was impossible she could love Graham, or that it was her duty to disobey her Father; the only thing at which she rather seemed to hesitate was our assertion that she must be attached to some other Person. For some time, she persevered in declaring that she knew no other young Man for whom she had the smallest Affection; but upon explaining the impossibility of such a thing she said that she beleived she *did like* Captain M'Kenzie better than any one she knew besides. This confession satisfied us and after having enumerated the good Qualities of M'Kenzie & assured her that she was violently in love with him, we desired to know whether he had ever in any wise declared his Affection to her.

"So far from having ever declared it, I have no reason to imagine that he has ever felt any for me." said Janetta. "That he certainly adores you (replied Sophia) there can be no doubt—. The Attachment must be reciprocal —. Did he never gaze on you with Admiration—tenderly press your hand—drop an involuntary tear—& leave the room abruptly?" "Never (replied She) that I remember —he has always left the room indeed when his visit has been ended, but has never gone away particularly abruptly or without making a bow." "Indeed my Love (said I) you must be mistaken—: for it is absolutely impossible that he should ever have left you but with Confusion, Despair, & Precipitation—. Consider but for a moment Janetta, & you must be convinced how absurd it is to suppose that he could ever make a Bow, or behave like any other Person." Having settled this Point to our satisfaction, the next we took into consideration was, to determine in what manner we should inform M'Kenzie of the favourable Opinion Janetta entertained of him.—. We at length agreed to acquaint him with it by an anony-

mous Letter which Sophia drew up in the following
Manner.

"Oh! happy Lover of the beautifull Janetta, oh! enviable Possessor of *her* Heart whose hand is destined to
another, why do you thus delay a confession of your
Attachment to the amiable Object of it? Oh! consider
that a few weeks will at once put an end to every flattering Hope that you may now entertain, by uniting the
unfortunate Victim of her father's Cruelty to the excre-
cable & detested Graham."

"Alas! why do you thus so cruelly connive at the pro-
jected Misery of her & of yourself by delaying to com-
municate that scheme which had doubtless long possessed
your imagination? A secret Union will at once secure
the felicity of both."

The amiable M'Kenzie, whose modesty as he afterwards assured us had been the only reason of his having
so long concealed the violence of his affection for Janetta,
on receiving this Billet flew on the wings of Love to
Macdonald-Hall, and so powerfully pleaded his Attachment to her who inspired it, that after a few more private
interveiws, Sophia & I experienced the Satisfaction of
seeing them depart for Gretna-Green, which they chose
for the celebration of their Nuptials, in preference to any
other place although it was at a considerable distance
from Macdonald-Hall.

Adeiu

Laura

Letter the 13th   Laura in Continuation

They had been gone nearly a couple of Hours, before
either Macdonald or Graham had entertained any suspicion of the affair—. And they might not even then have
suspected it, but for the following little Accident. Sophia
happening one Day to open a private Drawer in Macdonald's Library with one of her own keys, discovered

that it was the Place where he kept his Papers of consequence & amongst them some bank notes of considerable
amount. This discovery she imparted to me; and having
agreed together that it would be a proper treatment of
so vile a Wretch as Macdonald to deprive him of money,
perhaps dishonestly gained, it was determined that the
next time we should either of us happen to go that way,
we would take one or more of the Bank notes from the
drawer. This well-meant Plan we had often successfully
put in Execution; but alas! on the very day to Janetta's
Escape, as Sophia was majestically removing the 5th
Bank-note from the Drawer to her own purse, she was
suddenly most impertinently interrupted in her employment by the entrance of Macdonald himself, in a most
abrupt & precipitate Manner. Sophia (who though
naturally all winning sweetness could when occasions demanded it call forth the Dignity of her Sex) instantly put
on a most forbiding look, & darting an angry frown on
the undaunted Culprit, demanded in a haughty tone of
voice "Wherefore her retirement was thus insolently broken in on?" The unblushing Macdonald, without even
endeavouring to exculpate himself from the crime he was
charged with, meanly endeavoured to reproach Sophia
with ignobly defrauding him of his Money. The dignity
of Sophia was wounded; "Wretch (exclaimed she, hastily
replacing the Bank-note in the Drawer) how darest thou
to accuse me of an Act, of which the bare idea makes me
blush?" The base wretch was still unconvinced & continued to upbraid the justly-offended Sophia in such
opprobrious Language, that at length he so greatly provoked the gentle sweetness of her Nature, as to induce
her to revenge herself on him by informing him of
Janetta's Elopement, and of the active Part we had both
taken in the Affair. At this period of their Quarrel I
entered the Library and was as you may imagine equally
offended as Sophia at the ill-grounded Accusations of the
malevolent and contemptible Macdonald. "Base Mis-

creant (cried I) how canst thou thus undauntedly endeavour to sully the spotless reputation of such bright Excellence? Why dost thou not suspect *my* innocence as soon?" "Be satisfied Madam (replied he) I *do* suspect it, & therefore must desire that you will both leave this House in less than half an hour."

"We shall go willingly; (answered Sophia) our hearts have long detested thee, & nothing but our freindship for thy Daughter could have induced us to remain so long beneath thy roof."

"Your Freindship for my Daughter has indeed been most powerfully exerted by throwing her into the arms of an unprincipled Fortune-hunter." (replied he)

"Yes, (exclaimed I) amidst every misfortune, it will afford us some consolation to reflect that by this one act of Freindship to Janetta, we have amply discharged every obligation that we have received from her father."

"It must indeed be a most gratefull reflection, to your exalted minds." (said he.)

As soon as we had packed up our wardrobe & valuables, we left Macdonald Hall, & after having walked about a mile & a half we sate down by the side of a clear limpid stream to refresh our exhausted limbs. The place was suited to meditation.—. A Grove of full-grown Elms sheltered us from the East—. A Bed of full-grown Nettles from the West—. Before us ran the murmuring brook & behind us ran the turn-pike road. We were in a mood for contemplation & in a Disposition to enjoy so beautifull a spot. A mutual Silence which had for some time reigned between us, was at length broke by my exclaiming—"What a lovely Scene! Alas why are not Edward & Augustus here to enjoy its Beauties with us?".

"Ah! my beloved Laura (cried Sophia) for pity's sake forbear recalling to my remembrance the unhappy situation of my imprisoned Husband. Alas, what would I not give to learn the fate of my Augustus! to know if he is still in Newgate, or if he is yet hung. But never shall I

be able so far to conquer my tender sensibility as to en-
quire after him. Oh! do not I beseech you ever let me
again hear you repeat his beloved name—. It affects me
too deeply—. I cannot bear to hear him mentioned, it
wounds my feelings."

"Excuse me my Sophia for having thus unwillingly
offended you—" replied I—and then changing the conversation, desired her to admire the Noble Grandeur of
the Elms which Sheltered us from the Eastern Zephyr.
"Alas! my Laura (returned she) avoid so melancholy a
subject, I intreat you.— Do not again wound my Sensibility by Observations on those elms. They remind me of
Augustus—. He was like them, tall, magestic—he possessed that noble grandeur which you admire in them."

I was silent, fearfull lest I might any more unwillingly
distress her by fixing on any other subject of conversation
which might again remind her of Augustus.

"Why do you not speak my Laura?" (said she after a
short pause) "I cannot support this silence—you must
not leave me to my own reflections; they ever recur to
Augustus."

"What a beautifull Sky! (said I) How charmingly is
the azure varied by those delicate streaks of white!"

"Oh! my Laura (replied she hastily withdrawing her
Eyes from a momentary glance at the sky) do not thus
distress me by calling my Attention to an object which
so cruelly reminds me of my Augustus's blue sattin
Waistcoat striped with white! In pity to your unhappy
freind avoid a subject so distressing." What could I do?
The feelings of Sophia were at that time so exquisite, &
the tenderness she felt for Augustus so poignant that I
had not the power to start any other topic, justly fearing
that it might in some unforseen manner again awaken
all her sensibility by directing her thoughts to her Husband.— Yet to be silent would be cruel; She had intreated me to talk.

From this Dilemma I was most fortunately releived

by an accident truly apropos; it was the lucky overturn-
ing of a Gentleman's Phaeton, on the road which ran
murmuring behind us. It was a most fortunate Accident
as it diverted the Attention of Sophia from the melancholy reflections which she had been before indulging.
We instantly quitted our seats & ran to the rescue of
those who but a few moments before had been in so
elevated a situation as a fashionably high Phaeton, but
who were now laid low and sprawling in the Dust—.
"What an ample subject for reflection on the uncertain
Enjoyments of this World, would not that Phaeton & the
Life of Cardinal Wolsey afford a thinking Mind!" said
I to Sophia as we were hastening to the field of Action.

She had not time to answer me for every thought was
now engaged by the horrid Spectacle before us. Two
Gentlemen most elegantly attired but weltering in their
blood was what first struck our Eyes—we approached—
they were Edward & Augustus—Yes dearest Marianne
they were our Husbands. Sophia shreiked & fainted on
the Ground—I screamed and instantly ran mad—. We
remained thus mutually deprived of our Senses some
minutes, & on regaining them were deprived of them
again—. For an Hour & a Quarter did we continue in
this unfortunate Situation—Sophia fainting every moment & I running Mad as often. At length a Groan from
the hapless Edward (who alone retained any share of
Life) restored us to ourselves—. Had we indeed before
imagined that either of them lived, we should have been
more sparing of our Greif—but as we had supposed when
we first beheld them that they were no more, we knew
that nothing could remain to be done but what we were
about—. No sooner therefore did we hear my Edward's
groan than postponing our Lamentations for the present,
we hastily ran to the Dear Youth and kneeling on each
side of him implored him not to die—. "Laura (said He
fixing his now languid Eyes on me) I fear I have been
overturned."

I was overjoyed to find him yet sensible—.

"Oh! tell me Edward (said I) tell me I beseech you before you die, what has befallen you since that unhappy Day in which Augustus was arrested & we were separated—"

"I will" (said he) and instantly fetching a Deep sigh, expired—. Sophia immediately sunk again into a swoon—. *My* Greif was more audible My voice faltered, My Eyes assumed a vacant Stare, My face became as pale as Death, and my Senses were considerably impaired—.

"Talk not to me of Phaetons (said I, raving in a frantic, incoherent manner)—Give me a violin—. I'll play to him & sooth him in his melancholy Hours—Beware ye gentle Nymphs of Cupid's Thunderbolts, avoid the piercing Shafts of Jupiter—Look at that Grove of Firs— I see a Leg of Mutton—They told me Edward was not Dead; but they deceived me—they took him for a Cucumber—" Thus I continued wildly exclaiming on my Edward's death—. For two Hours did I rave thus madly and should not then have left off, as I was not in the least fatigued, had not Sophia who was just recovered from her swoon, intreated me to consider that Night was now approaching and that the Damps began to fall. "And whither shall we go (said I) to shelter us from either"? "To that white Cottage." (replied she pointing to a neat building which rose up amidst the Grove of Elms & which I had not before observed—) I agreed & we instantly walked to it—we knocked at the door—it was opened by an old Woman; on being requested to afford us a Night's Lodging, she informed us that her House was but small, that she had only two Bed-rooms, but that However we should be wellcome to one of them. We were satisfied & followed the good Woman into the House where we were greatly cheered by the sight of a comfortable fire—. She was a Widow & had only one Daughter, who was then just Seventeen—One of the best of ages; but alas! she was very plain & her name was Bridget. . . . . . Nothing therefore could be expected from her—she could not be supposed to possess either exalted Ideas, Delicate Feelings or refined Sensibilities—She was nothing more than a mere good-tempered, civil & obliging Young Woman; as such we could scarcely dislike her —she was only an Object of Contempt—.

Adeiu

Laura

Letter the 14th   Laura in continuation

Arm yourself my amiable Young Freind with all the philosophy you are Mistress of; summon up all the fortitude you possess, for Alas! in the perusal of the following Pages your sensibility will be most severely tried. Ah! what were the Misfortunes I had before experienced & which I have already related to you, to the one I am now going to inform you of. The Death of my Father my Mother, and my Husband though almost more than my gentle Nature could support, were trifles in comparison to the misfortune I am now proceeding to relate. The morning after our arrival at the Cottage, Sophia complained of a violent pain in her delicate limbs, accompanied with a disagreable Head-ake. She attributed it to a cold caught by her continued faintings in the open Air as the Dew was falling the Evening before. This I feared was but too probably the case; since how could it be otherwise accounted for that I should have escaped the same indisposition but, by supposing that the bodily Exertions I had undergone in my repeated fits of frenzy, had so effectually circulated & warmed my Blood as to make me proof against the chilling Damps of Night, whereas, Sophia lying totally inactive on the Ground must have been exposed to all their Severity. I was most seriously alarmed by her illness which trifling as it may appear to you, a certain instinctive Sensibility whispered me, would in the End be fatal to her.

Alas! my fears were but too fully justified; she grew gradually worse & I daily became more alarmed for her. —At length she was obliged to confine herself solely to the Bed allotted us by our worthy Landlady—. Her disorder turned to a galloping Consumption & in a few Days carried her off. Amidst all my Lamentations for her (& violent you may suppose they were) I yet received some consolation in the reflection of my having paid every Attention to her, that could be offered, in her illness. I had wept over her every Day—had bathed her sweet face with my tears & had pressed her fair Hands continually in mine—. "My beloved Laura (said she to me a few Hours before she died) take warning from my unhappy End & avoid the imprudent conduct which has occasioned it . . beware of fainting-fits . . Though at the time they may be refreshing & Agreable yet beleive me they will in the end, if too often repeated & at improper seasons, prove destructive to your Constitution . . . . . My fate will teach you this . . I die a Martyr to my greif for the loss of Augustus . . . . One fatal swoon has cost me my Life . . . . Beware of swoons Dear Laura . . . A frenzy fit is not one quarter so pernicious; it is an exercise to the Body & if not too violent, is I dare say conducive to Health in its consequences—Run mad as often as you chuse; but do not faint—".

These were the last words she ever adressed to me . . . It was her dieing Advice to her afflicted Laura, who has ever most faithfully adhered to it.

After having attended my lamented freind to her Early Grave, I immediately (tho' late at night) left the detested Village in which she died, & near which had expired my Husband & Augustus. I had not walked many yards from it before I was overtaken by a Stage-Coach, in which I instantly took a place, determined to proceed in it to Edinburgh, where I hoped to find some kind pitying

Freind who would receive and comfort me in my Afflictions.

It was so dark when I entered the Coach that I could not distinguish the Number of my Fellow-travellers; I could only perceive that there were Many. Regardless however of any thing concerning them, I gave myself up to my own sad Reflections. A general Silence prevailed —A Silence, which was by nothing interrupted but by the loud & repeated snores of one of the Party.

"What an illiterate villain must that Man be! (thought I to myself) What a total Want of delicate refinement must he have who can thus shock our senses by such a brutal Noise! He must I am certain be capable of every bad Action! There is no crime too black for such a Character!" Thus reasoned I within myself, & doubtless such were the reflections of my fellow travellers.

At length, returning Day enabled me to behold the unprincipled Scoundrel who had so violently disturbed my feelings. It was Sir Edward the father of my Deceased Husband. By his side, sate Augusta, & on the same seat with me were your Mother & Lady Dorothea. Imagine my Surprise at finding myself thus seated amongst my old Acquaintance. Great as was my astonishment, it was yet increased, when on look out of Windows, I beheld the Husband of Philippa. with Philippa by his side, on the Coach-box, & when on looking behind, I beheld, Philander & Gustavus in the Basket. "Oh! Heavens, (exclaimed I) is it possible that I should so unexpectedly be surrounded by my nearest Relations and Connections"? These words roused the rest of the Party, and every eye was directed to the corner in which I sat. "Oh! my Isabel (continued I throwing myself across Lady Dorothea into her arms) receive once more to your Bosom the unfortunate Laura. Alas! when we last parted in the Vale of Usk, I was happy in being united to the best of Edwards; I had then a Father and a Mother, & had never known misfortunes—But now deprived of every freind but you—."

"What! (interrupted Augusta) is my Brother dead then? Tell us I intreat you what is become of him?" "Yes, cold & insensible Nymph, (replied I) that luckless Swain your Brother, is no more, & you may now glory in being the Heiress of Sir Edward's fortune."

Although I had always despised her from the Day I had overheard her conversation with my Edward, yet in civility I complied with hers & Sir Edward's intreaties that I would inform them of the whole melancholy Affair. They were greatly shocked—Even the obdurate Heart of Sir Edward & the insensible one of Augusta, were touched with Sorrow, by the unhappy tale. At the request of your Mother I related to them every other misfortune which had befallen me since we parted. Of the imprisonment of Augustus & the absence of Edward —of our arrival in Scotland—of our unexpected Meeting with our Grand-father and our cousins—of our visit to Macdonald-Hall—of the singular Service we there performed towards Janetta—of her Fathers ingratitude for it . . . . . of his inhuman Behaviour, unaccountable suspicions, & barbarous treatment of us, in obliging us to leave the House . . . . . of our Lamentations on the loss of Edward & Augustus & finally of the melancholy Death of my beloved Companion.

Pity & Surprise were strongly depictured in your Mother's Countenance, during the whole of my narration, but I am sorry to say, that to the eternal reproach of her Sensibility, the latter infinitely predominated. Nay, faultless as my Conduct had certainly been during the whole Course of my late Misfortunes & Adventures, she pretended to find fault with my Behaviour in many of the situations in which I had been placed. As I was sensible myself, that I had always behaved in a manner which reflected Honour on my Feelings & Refinement, I paid little attention to what she said, & desired her to satisfy my Curiosity by informing me how she came there, instead of wounding my spotless reputation with unjustifiable Reproaches. As soon as she had complyed with my wishes in this particular & had given me an accurate detail of every thing that had befallen her since our separation (the particulars of which if you are not already acquainted with, your Mother will give you) I applied to Augusta for the same information respecting herself, Sir Edward & Lady Dorothea.

She told me that having a considerable taste for the Beauties of Nature, her curiosity to behold the delightful scenes it exhibited in that part of the World had been so much raised by Gilpin's Tour to the Highlands, that she had prevailed on her Father to undertake a Tour of Scotland & had persuaded Lady Dorothea to accompany them. That they had arrived at Edinburgh a few days before & from thence had made daily Excursions into the Country around in the Stage Coach they were then in, from one of which Excursions they were at that time returning. My next enquiries were concerning Philippa & her Husband, the latter of whom I learned having spent all her fortune, had recourse for subsistance to the talent in which, he had always most excelled, namely, Driving, & that having sold every thing which belonged to them except their Coach, had converted it into a Stage, & in order to be removed from any of his former Acquaintance, had driven it to Edinburgh from whence he went to Sterling every other Day; That Philippa still retaining her affection for her ungratefull Husband, had followed him to Scotland & generally accompanied him in his little Excursions to Sterling. "It has only been to throw a little money into their Pockets (continued Augusta) that my Father has always travelled in their Coach to veiw the beauties of the Country since our arrival in Scotland—for it would certainly have been much more agreable to us, to visit the Highlands in a Postchaise than merely to travel from Edinburgh to Sterling & from Sterling to Edinburgh every other Day in a crouded & uncomfortable Stage." I perfectly agreed with her in her sentiments on the Affair, & secretly blamed Sir Edward for thus sacrificing his Daughter's pleasure for the sake of a ridiculous old Woman whose folly in marrying so young a Man ought to be punished. His Behaviour however was entirely of a piece with his general Character; for what could be expected from a Man who possessed not the smallest atom of Sensibility, who scarcely knew the meaning of Simpathy, & who actually snored—.

Adeiu

Laura

Letter the 15th   Laura in continuation

When we arrived at the town where we were to Breakfast, I was determined to speak with Philander & Gustavus, & to that purpose as soon as I left the Carriage, I went to the Basket & tenderly enquired after their Health, expressing my fears of the uneasiness of their Situation. At first they seemed rather confused at my Appearance dreading no doubt that I might call them to account for the money which our Grandfather had left me & which they had unjustly deprived me of, but finding that I mentioned nothing of the Matter, they desired me to step into the Basket as we might there converse with greater ease. Accordingly I entered & whilst the rest of the party were devouring Green tea & buttered toast, we feasted ourselves in a more refined & Sentimental Manner by a confidential Conversation. I informed them of every thing which had befallen me during the course of my Life, and at my request they related to me every incident of theirs.

"We are the sons as you already know, of the two youngest Daughters which Lord St. Clair had by Laurina an italian opera girl. Our mothers could neither of them exactly ascertain who were our fathers; though it is generally beleived that Philander, is the son of one Philip

Jones a Bricklayer and that my father was Gregory
Staves a Staymaker of Edinburgh. This is however of
little consequence, for as our Mothers were certainly
never married to either of them, it reflects no Dishonour
on our Blood which is of a most ancient & unpolluted
kind. Bertha (the Mother of Philander) & Agatha (my
own Mother) always lived together. They were neither
of them very rich; their united fortunes had originally
amounted to nine thousand Pounds, but as they had always lived upon the principal of it, when we were fifteen
it was diminished to nine Hundred. This nine Hundred,
they always kept in a Drawer in one of the Tables which
stood in our common sitting Parlour, for the Convenience
of having it always at Hand. Whether it was from this
circumstance, of its being easily taken, or from a wish of
being independant, or from an excess of Sensibility (for
which we are always remarkable) I cannot now determine, but certain it is that when we had reached our
15th year, we took the Nine Hundred Pounds & ran
away. Having obtained this prize we were determined
to manage it with economy & not to spend it either
with folly or Extravagance. To this purpose we therefore
divided it into nine parcels, one of which we devoted to
Victuals, the 2d to Drink, the 3d to Housekeeping, the
4th to Carriages, the 5th to Horses, the 6th to Servants,
the 7th to Amusements, the 8th to Cloathes & the 9th
to Silver Buckles. Having thus arranged our Expences
for two Months (for we expected to make the nine Hundred Pounds last as long) we hastened to London & had
the good luck to spend it in 7 weeks & a Day which was
6 Days sooner than we had intended. As soon as we had
thus happily disencumbered ourselves from the weight
of so much Money, we began to think of returning to our
Mothers, but accidentally hearing that they were both
starved to death, we gave over the design & determined
to engage ourselves to some strolling Company of Players,
as we had always a turn for the Stage. Accordingly we

offered our services to one & were accepted; our Company was indeed rather small, as it consisted only of the Manager his wife & ourselves, but there were fewer to pay and the only inconvenience attending it was the Scarcity of Plays which for want of People to fill the Characters, we could perform.—. We did not mind trifles however—. One of our most admired Performances was *Macbeth*, in which we were truly great. The Manager always played *Banquo* himself, his Wife my *Lady Macbeth*. I did the *Three Witches* & Philander acted *all the rest*. To say the truth this tragedy was not only the Best, but the only Play we ever performed; & after having acted it all over England, and Wales, we came to Scotland to exhibit it over the remainder of Great Britain. We happened to be quartered in that very Town, where you came and met your Grandfather—. We were in the Inn-yard when his Carriage entered & perceiving by the Arms to whom it belonged, & knowing that Lord St. Clair was our Grandfather, we agreed to endeavour to get something from him by discovering the Relationship—. You know how well it succeeded—. Having obtained the two Hundred Pounds, we instantly left the Town, leaving our Manager & his wife to act *Macbeth* by themselves, & took the road to Sterling, where we spent our little fortune with great *eclat*. We are now returning to Edinburgh to get some preferment in the Acting way; & such my Dear Cousin is our History."

I thanked the amiable Youth for his entertaining Narration, & after expressing my Wishes for their Welfare & Happiness, left them in their little Habitation & returned to my other Freinds who impatiently expected me.

My Adventures are now drawing to a close my dearest Marianne; at least for the present.

When we arrived at Edinburgh Sir Edward told me that as the Widow of his Son, he desired I would accept from his Hands of four Hundred a year. I graciously promised that I would, but could not help observing that the unsimpathetic Baronet offered it more on account of my being the Widow of Edward than in being the refined & Amiable Laura.

I took up my Residence in a romantic Village in the Highlands of Scotland, where I have ever since continued, & where I can uninterrupted by unmeaning Visits, indulge in a melancholy solitude, my unceasing Lamentations for the Death of my Father, my Mother, my Husband & my Freind.

Augusta has been for several Years united to Graham the Man of all others most suited to her; she became acquainted with him during her stay in Scotland.

Sir Edward in hopes of gaining an Heir to his Title & Estate, at the same time married Lady Dorothea—. His wishes have been answered.

Philander & Gustavus, after having raised their reputation by their Performances in the Theatrical Line at Edinburgh, removed to Covent Garden, where they still Exhibit under the assumed names of *Lewis* & *Quick*.

Philippa has long paid the Debt of Nature, Her Husband however still continues to drive the Stage-Coach from Edinburgh to Sterling:—

Adeiu my Dearest Marianne.

Laura

Finis

June 13th 1790

LESLEY CASTLE

AN UNFINISHED NOVEL IN LETTERS

To Henry Thomas Austen Esqre.

Sir

I am now availing myself of the Liberty you have frequently honoured me with of dedicating one of my Novels to you. That it is unfinished, I greive; yet fear that from me, it will always remain so; that as far as it is carried, it Should be so trifling and so unworthy of you, is another concern to your obliged humble

Servant
The Author

Messrs Demand & Co—please to pay Jane Austen Spinster the sum of one hundred guineas on account of your Humbl. Servant.

H T Austen

£105. 0. 0

Letter The first is from
Miss Margaret Lesley to Miss Charlotte
Lutterell.

Lesley-Castle

Janry 3d—1792.

My Brother has just left us. "Matilda (said he at parting)
you and Margaret will I am certain take all the care of
my dear little one, that she might have received from an
indulgent, an affectionate an amiable Mother." Tears
rolled down his cheeks as he spoke these words—the remembrance of her, who had so wantonly disgraced the
Maternal character and so openly violated the conjugal
Duties, prevented his adding anything farther; he em-
braced his sweet Child and after saluting Matilda & Me
hastily broke from us and seating himself in his Chaise,
pursued the road to Aberdeen. Never was there a better
young Man! Ah! how little did he deserve the misfortunes he has experienced in the Marriage state. So good
a Husband to so bad a Wife! for you know my dear
Charlotte that the Worthless Louisa left him, her Child
& reputation a few weeks ago in company with Danvers
&* dishonour. Never was there a sweeter face, a finer
form, or a less amiable Heart than Louisa owned! Her
child already possesses the personal charms of her unhappy Mother! May she inherit from her Father all his
mental ones! Lesley is at present but five and twenty,
and has already given himself up to melancholy and
Despair; what a difference between him and his Father!
Sir George is 57 and still remains the Beau, the flightly
stripling, the gay Lad and sprightly Youngster, that his
Son was really about five years back, and that *he* has
affected to appear ever since my remembrance. While

*Rakehelly Dishonour Esqre.

our father is fluttering about the streets of London, gay, dissipated, and Thoughtless at the age of 57, Matilda and I continue secluded from Mankind in our old and Mouldering Castle, which is situated two miles from Perth on a bold projecting Rock, and commands an extensive view of the Town and its delightful Environs. But tho' retired from almost all the World, (for we visit no one but the M'Leods, the M'Kenzies, the M'Phersons, the M'Cartneys, the M'donalds, The M'Kinnons, the M'lellans, the M'Kays, the Macbeths and the Macduffs) we are neither dull nor unhappy; on the contrary there never were two more lively, more agreable or more witty Girls, than we are; not an hour in the Day hangs heavy on our hands. We read, we work, we walk and when fatigued with these Employments releive our spirits, either by a lively song, a graceful Dance, or by some smart bon-mot, and witty repartée. We are handsome my dear Charlotte, very handsome and the greatest of our Perfections is, that we are entirely insensible of them ourselves. But why do I thus dwell on myself? Let me rather repeat the praise of our dear little Neice the innocent Louisa, who is at present sweetly smiling in a gentle Nap, as she reposes on the Sofa. The dear Creature is just turned of two years old; as handsome as tho' 2 & 20, as sensible as tho' 2 & 30, and as prudent as tho' 2 & 40. To convince you of this, I must inform you that she has a very fine complexion and very pretty features, that she already knows the two first letters in the Alphabet, and that she never tears her frocks—. If I have not now convinced you of her Beauty, Sense & Prudence, I have nothing more to urge in support of my assertion, and you will therefore have no way of deciding the Affair but by coming to Lesley Castle, and by a personal acquaintance with Louisa, determine for yourself. Ah! my dear Freind, how happy should I be to see you within these venerable Walls! It is now four years since my removal from School has separated me from you; that two

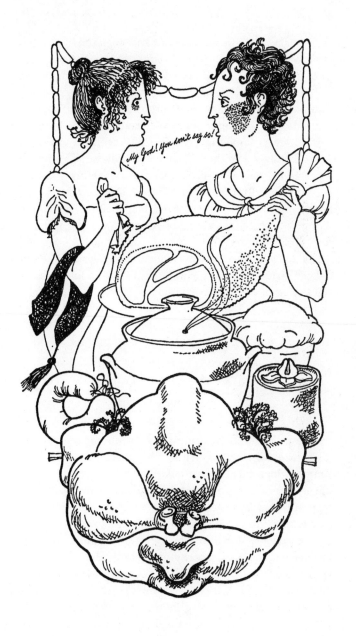

such tender Hearts, so closely linked together by the ties
of simpathy and Freindship, should be so widely removed
from each other, is vastly moving. I live in Perthshire,
You in Sussex. We might meet in London, were my
Father disposed to carry me there, and were your Mother
to be there at the same time. We might meet at Bath, at
Tunbridge, or anywhere else indeed, could we but be at
the same place together. We have only to hope that such
a period may arrive. My Father does not return to us till
Autumn; my Brother will leave Scotland in a few Days;
he is impatient to travel. Mistaken Youth! He vainly
flatters himself that change of Air will heal the Wounds
of a broken Heart! You will join with me I am certain
my dear Charlotte, in prayers for the recovery of the unhappy Lesley's peace of Mind, which must ever be essential to that of your sincere freind

M. Lesley

Letter the second
From Miss C. Lutterell to Miss M.
Lesley in answer

Glenford

Feb:ry 12

I have a thousand excuses to beg for having so long de-
layed thanking you my dear Peggy for your agreable
Letter, which beleive me I should not have deferred doing, had not every moment of my time during the last
five weeks been so fully employed in the necessary ar-
rangements for my sisters Wedding, as to allow me no
time to devote either to you or myself. And now what
provokes me more than anything else is that the Match
is broke off, and all my Labour thrown away. Imagine
how great the Dissapointment must be to me, when you
consider that after having laboured both by Night and
Day, in order to get the Wedding dinner ready by the
time appointed, after having roasted Beef, Broiled Mut-

ton, and Stewed Soup enough to last the new-married Couple through the Honey-moon, I had the mortification of finding that I had been Roasting, Broiling and Stewing both the Meat and Myself to no purpose. Indeed my dear Freind, I never remember suffering any vexation equal to what I experienced on last Monday when my Sister came running to me in the Store-room with her face as White as a Whipt syllabub, and told me that Hervey had been thrown from his Horse, had fractured his Scull and was pronounced by his Surgeon to be in the most emminent Danger. "Good God! (said I) you dont say so? Why what in the name of Heaven will become of all the Victuals? We shall never be able to eat it while it is good. However, we'll call in the Surgeon to help us—. I shall be able to manage the Sir-loin myself; my Mother will eat the Soup, and You and the Doctor must finish the rest." Here I was interrupted, by seeing my poor Sister fall down to appearance Lifeless upon one of the Chests, where we keep our Table linen. I immediately called my Mother and the Maids, and at last we brought her to herself again; as soon as ever she was sensible, she expressed a determination of going instantly to Henry, and was so wildly bent on this Scheme, that we had the greatest Difficulty in the World to prevent her putting it in execution; at last however more by Force than Entreaty we prevailed on her to go into her room; we laid her upon the Bed, and she continued for some Hours in the most dreadful Convulsions. My Mother and I continued in the room with her, and when any intervals of tolerable Composure in Eloisa would allow us, we joined in heartfelt lamentations on the dreadful Waste in our provisions which this Event must occasion, and in concerting some plan for getting rid of them. We agreed that the best thing we could do was to begin eating them immediately, and accordingly we ordered up the cold Ham and Fowls, and instantly began our Devouring Plan on them with great Alacrity. We would have persuaded Eloisa to have taken a Wing of a Chicken, but she would not be persuaded. She was however much quieter than she had been; the Convulsions she had before suffered having given way to an almost perfect Insensibility. We endeavoured to rouse her by every means in our power, but to no purpose. I talked to her of Henry. "Dear Eloisa (said I) there's no occasion for your crying so much about such a trifle. (for I was willing to make light of it in order to comfort her) I beg you would not mind it—. You see it does not vex me in the least; though perhaps *I* may suffer most from it after all; for I shall not only be obliged to eat up all the Victuals I have dressed already, but must if Hervey should recover (which however is not very likely) dress as much for you again; or should he die (as I suppose he will) I shall still have to prepare a Dinner for you whenever you marry any one else. So you see that tho' perhaps for the present it may afflict you to think of Henry's sufferings, Yet I dare say he'll die soon, and then his pain will be over and you will be easy, whereas my Trouble will last much longer for work hard as I may, I am certain that the pantry cannot be cleared in less than a fortnight." Thus I did all in my power to console her, but without any effect, and at last as I saw that she did not seem to listen to me, I said no more, but leaving her with my Mother I took down the remains of The Ham & Chicken, and sent William to ask how Hervey did. He was not expected to live many Hours; he died the same day. We took all possible care to break the Melancholy Event to Eloisa in the tenderest manner; yet in spite of every precaution, her Sufferings on hearing it were too violent for her reason, and she continued for many hours in a high Delirium. She is still extremely ill, and her Physicians are greatly afraid of her going into a Decline. We are therefore preparing for Bristol, where we mean to be in the course of the next week. And now my dear Margaret let me talk a little of your affairs; and in the first place I

must inform you that it is confidiently reported, your
Father is going to be married; I am very unwilling to beleive so unpleasing a report, and at the same time cannot
wholly discredit it. I have written to my friend Susan
Fitzgerald, for information concerning it, which as she is
at present in Town, she will be very able to give me. I
know not who is the Lady. I think your Brother is extremely right in the resolution he has taken of travelling,
as it will perhaps contribute to obliterate from his remembrance, those disagreable Events, which have lately
so much afflicted him—I am happy to find that tho' secluded from all the World, neither you nor Matilda are
dull or unhappy—that you may never know what it is
to be either is the wish of your sincerely Affectionate

C.L.

P.S. I have this instant received an answer from my
freind Susan, which I enclose to you, and on which you
will make your own reflections.

The enclosed Letter

My dear Charlotte

You could not have applied for information concerning
the report of Sir George Lesleys Marriage, to anyone
better able to give it you than I am. Sir George is certainly married; I was myself present at the Ceremony,
which you will not be surprised at when I subscribe myself your

Affectionate
Susan Lesley

Letter the third
From Miss Margaret Lesley to Miss C.
Lutterell

Lesley Castle
February the 16th

I *have* made my own reflections on the letter you en-
closed to me, my Dear Charlotte and I will now tell you

what those reflections were. I reflected that if by this
second Marriage Sir George should have a second family,
our fortunes must be considerably diminushed—that if
his Wife should be of an extravagant turn, she would encourage him to persevere in that Gay & Dissipated way
of Life to which little encouragement would be necessary,
and which has I fear already proved but too detrimental
to his health and fortune—that she would now become
Mistress of those Jewels which once adorned our Mother,
and which Sir George had always promised us—that if
they did not come into Perthshire I should not be able
to gratify my curiosity of beholding my Mother-in-law,
and that if they did, Matilda would no longer sit at the
head of her Father's table—. These my dear Charlotte
were the melancholy reflections which crouded into my
imagination after perusing Susan's letter to you, and
which instantly ocurred to Matilda when she had per-
used it likewise. The same ideas, the same fears, immediately occupied her Mind, and I know not which reflection distressed her most, whether the probable Di-
minution of our Fortunes, or her own Consequence. We
both wish very much to know whether Lady Lesley is
handsome & what is your opinion of her; as you honour
her with the appellation of your freind, we flatter ourselves that she must be amiable. My Brother is already
in Paris. He intends to quit it in a few Days, and to begin
his route to Italy. He writes in a most chearfull Manner,
says that the air of France has greatly recovered both his
Health and Spirits; that he has now entirely ceased to
think of Louisa with any degree either of Pity or Affection, that he even feels himself obliged to her for her
Elopement, as he thinks it very good fun to be single
again. By this, you may perceive that he has entirely re-
gained that chearful Gaiety, and sprightly Wit, for which
he was once so remarkable. When he first became acquainted with Louisa which was little more than three
years ago, he was one of the most lively, the most agre-

able young Men of the age—. I beleive you never yet heard the particulars of his first acquaintance with her. It commenced at our cousin Colonel Drummond's, at whose house in Cumberland he spent the Christmas, in which he attained the age of two and twenty. Louisa Burton was the Daughter of a distant Relation of Mrs. Drummond, who dieing a few Months before in extreme poverty, left his only Child then about eighteen to the protection of any of his Relations who would protect her. Mrs. Drummond was the only one who found herself so disposed—Louisa was therefore removed from a miserable Cottage in Yorkshire to an elegant Mansion in Cumberland, and from every pecuniary Distress that Poverty could inflict, to every elegant Enjoyment that Money could purchase—. Louisa was naturally ill-tempered and Cunning; but she had been taught to disguise her real Disposition, under the appearance of insinuating Sweetness by a father who but too well knew, that to be married, would be the only chance she would have of not being starved, and who flattered himself that with such an extraordinary share of personal beauty, joined to a gentleness of Manners, and an engaging address, she might stand a good chance of pleasing some young Man who might afford to marry a Girl without a Shilling. Louisa perfectly entered into her father's schemes and was determined to forward them with all her care & attention. By dint of Perseverance and Application, she had at length so thoroughly disguised her natural disposition under the mask of Innocence, and Softness, as to impose upon every one who had not by a long and constant intimacy with her discovered her real Character. Such was Louisa when the hapless Lesley first beheld her at Drummond-house. His heart which (to use your favourite comparison) was as delicate as sweet and as tender as a Whipt-syllabub, could not resist her attractions. In a very few Days, he was falling in love, shortly afterwards actually fell, and before he had known her a

Month, he had married her. My Father was at first
highly displeased at so hasty and imprudent a connection;
but when he found that they did not mind it, he soon
became perfectly reconciled to the match. The Estate
near Aberdeen which my brother possesses by the bounty
of his great Uncle independant of Sir George, was entirely
sufficient to support him and my Sister in Elegance &
Ease. For the first twelvemonth, no one could be happier
than Lesley, and no one more amiable to appearance
than Louisa, and so plausibly did She act and so cauti-
ously behave that tho' Matilda and I often spent several
weeks together with them, yet we neither of us had any
suspicion of her real Disposition. After the birth of Louisa
however, which one would have thought would have
strengthened her regard for Lesley, the mask she had so
long supported was by degrees thrown aside, and as probably she then thought herself secure in the affection of
her Husband (which did indeed appear if possible aug-
mented by the birth of his Child) She seemed to take no
pains to prevent that affection from ever diminushing.
Our visits therefore to Dunbeath, were now less frequent
and by far less agreable than they used to be. Our absence was however never either mentioned or lamented
by Louisa who in the society of the young Danvers with
whom she became acquainted at Aberdeen (he was at
one of the Universities there,) felt infinitely happier than
in that of Matilda and your freind, tho' there certainly
never were pleasanter Girls than we are. You know the
sad end of all Lesleys connubial happiness; I will not repeat it—. Adeiu my dear Charlotte; although I have not
yet mentioned any thing of the matter, I hope you will
do me the justice to believe that I *think* and *feel*, a great
deal for your Sisters affliction. I do not doubt but that
the healthy air of the Bristol downs, will intirely remove
it, by erasing from her Mind the remembrance of Henry.

　　　　　　　I am my dear Charlotte yrs ever
　　　　　　　　　　　ML—.

Letter the fourth
From Miss C. Lutterell to Miss M.
Lesley

Bristol

February 27th

My dear Peggy

I have but just received your letter, which being directed
to Sussex while I was at Bristol was obliged to be for-
warded to me here, & from some unaccountable Delay,
has but this instant reached me—. I return you many
thanks for the account it contains of Lesley's acquaintance, Love & Marriage with Louisa, which has not the
less entertained me for having often been repeated to me
before.

I have the satisfaction of informing you that we have
every reason to imagine our pantry is by this time nearly
cleared, as we left particular orders with the Servants to
eat as hard as they possibly could, and to call in a couple
of Chairwomen to assist them. We brought a cold Pigeon
pye, a cold turkey, a cold tongue, and half a dozen Jellies
with us, which we were lucky enough with the help of
our Landlady, her husband, and their three children, to
get rid of, in less than two days after our arrival. Poor
Eloisa is still so very indifferent both in Health & Spirits,
that I very much fear, the air of the Bristol downs,
healthy as it is, has not been able to drive poor Henry
from her remembrance.

You ask me whether your new Mother in law is handsome & amiable—I will now give you an exact description of her bodily and mental charms. She is short, and
extremely well-made; is naturally pale, but rouges a
good deal; has fine eyes, and fine teeth, as she will take
care to let you know as soon as she sees you, and is alto-
gether very pretty. She is remarkably good-tempered
when she has her own way, and very lively when she is
not out of humour. She is naturally extravagant and not

very affected; she never reads anything but the letters she receives from me, and never writes anything but her answers to them. She plays, sings & Dances, but has no taste for either, and excells in none, tho' she says she is passionately fond of all. Perhaps you may flatter me so far as to be surprised that one of whom I speak with so little affection should be my particular freind; but to tell you the truth, our freindship arose rather from Caprice on her side than Esteem on mine. We spent two or three days together with a Lady in Berkshire with whom we both happened to be connected—. During our visit, the Weather being remarkably bad, and our party particularly stupid, she was so good as to conceive a violent partiality for me, which very soon settled in a downright Freindship, and ended in an established correspondence. She is probably by this time as tired of me, as I am of her; but as she is too polite and I am too civil to say so, our letters are still as frequent and affectionate as ever, and our Attachment as firm and sincere as when it first commenced.— As she had a great taste for the pleasures of London, and of Brighthelmstone, she will I dare say find some difficulty in prevailing on herself ever to satisfy the curiosity I dare say she feels of beholding you, at the expence of quitting those favourite haunts of Dissipation, for the melancholy tho' venerable gloom of the castle you inhabit. Perhaps however if she finds her health impaired by too much amusement, she may acquire fortitude sufficient to undertake a Journey to Scotland in the hope of its proving at least beneficial to her health, if not conducive to her happiness. Your fears I am sorry to say, concerning your fathers extravagance, your own fortunes, your Mothers Jewels and your Sister's consequence, I should suppose are but too well founded. My freind herself has four thousand pounds, and will probably spend nearly as much every year in Dress and Public places, if she can get it—she will certainly not endeavour to reclaim Sir George from the manner of living to which he has been so long accustomed, and there is therefore some reason to fear that you will be very well off, if you get any fortune at all. The Jewels I should imagine too will undoubtedly be hers, & there is too much reason to think that she will reside at her Husbands table in preference to his Daughter. But as so melancholy a subject must necessarily extremely distress you, I will no longer dwell on it—.

Eloisa's indisposition has brought us to Bristol at so unfashionable a season of the year, that we have actually seen but one genteel family since we came. Mr & Mrs Marlowe are very agreable people; the ill health of their little boy occasioned their arrival here; you may imagine that being the only family with whom we can converse, we are of course on a footing of intimacy with them; we see them indeed almost every day, and dined with them yesterday. We spent a very pleasant Day, and had a very good Dinner, tho' to be sure the Veal was terribly underdone, and the Curry had no seasoning. I could not help wishing all dinner-time that I had been at the dressing it—. A brother of Mrs Marlowe, Mr Cleveland is with them at present; he is a good-looking young Man, and seems to have a good deal to say for himself. I tell Eloisa that she should set her cap at him, but she does not at all seem to relish the proposal. I should like to see the girl married and Cleveland has a very good estate. Perhaps you may wonder that I do not consider *myself* as well as my Sister in my matrimonial Projects; but to tell you the truth I never wish to act a more principal part at a Wedding than the superintending and directing the Dinner, and therefore while I can get any of my acquaintance to marry for me, I shall never think of doing it myself, as I very much suspect that I should not have so much time for dressing my own Wedding-dinner, as for dressing that of my freinds.

Yrs sincerely

CL

Letter the fifth
Miss Margaret Lesley to Miss Charlotte
Lutterell

Lesley-Castle

March 18th

On the same day that I received your last kind letter, Matilda received one from Sir George which was dated from Edinburgh, and informed us that he should do himself the pleasure of introducing Lady Lesley to us on the following evening. This as you may suppose considerably surprised us, particularly as your account of her Ladyship had given us reason to imagine there was little chance of her visiting Scotland at a time that London must be so gay. As it was our business however to be delighted at such a mark of condescension as a visit from Sir George and Lady Lesley, we prepared to return them an answer expressive of the happiness we enjoyed in expectation of such a Blessing, when luckily recollecting that as they were to reach the Castle the next Evening, it would be impossible for my father to receive it before he left Edinburgh, We contented ourselves with leaving them to suppose that we were as happy as we ought to be. At nine in the Evening on the following day, they came, accompanied by one of Lady Lesleys brothers. Her Ladyship perfectly answers the description you sent me of her, except that I do not think her so pretty as you seem to consider her. She has not a bad face, but there is something so extremely unmajestic in her little diminutive figure, as to render her in comparison with the elegant height of Matilda and Myself, an insignificant Dwarf. Her curiosity to see us (which must have been great to bring her more than four hundred miles) being now perfectly gratified, she already begins to mention their return to town, and has desired us to accompany her—. We cannot refuse her request since it is seconded by the commands of our Father, and thirded by the en-

treaties of Mr Fitzgerald who is certainly one of the most
pleasing young Men, I ever beheld, It is not yet determined when we are to go, but when ever we do we shall
certainly take our little Louisa with us. Adeiu my dear
Charlotte; Matilda unites in best Wishes to You &
Eloisa, with your ever

ML

Letter the sixth
Lady Lesley to Miss Charlotte
Lutterell

Lesley-Castle

March 20th

We arrived here my sweet Freind about a fortnight ago,
and I already heartily repent that I ever left our charming House in Portman-Square for such a dismal old
weather-beaten Castle as this. You can form no idea
sufficiently hideous, of its dungeon-like form. It is actually perched upon a Rock to appearance so totally in-
accessible, that I expected to have been pulled up by a
rope; and sincerely repented having gratified my curiosity to behold my Daughters at the expence of being
obliged to enter their prison in so dangerous & ridiculous
a Manner. But as soon as I once found myself safely
arrived in the inside of this tremendous building, I com-
forted myself with the hope of having my spirits revived,
by the sight of the two beautiful Girls, such as the Miss
Lesleys had been represented to me, at Edinburgh. But
here again, I met with nothing but Disapointment and
Surprise. Matilda and Margaret Lesley are two great,
tall, out of the way, over-grown Girls, just of a proper
size to inhabit a Castle almost as Large in comparison
as themselves. I wish my dear Charlotte that you could
but behold these Scotch Giants; I am sure they would
frighten you out of your wits. They will do very well as
foils to myself, so I have invited them to accompany me

to London where I hope to be in the course of a fortnight. Besides these two fair Damsels, I found a little humoured Brat here who I believe is some relation to them; they told me who she was, and gave me a long rigmerole story of her father and Miss *Somebody* which I have entirely forgot. I hate Scandal and detest Children.—. I have been plagued ever since I came here with tiresome visits from a parcel of Scotch wretches, with terrible hard names; they were so civil, gave me so many invitations, and talked of coming again so soon, that I could not help affronting them. I suppose I shall not see them any more, and yet as a family party we are so stupid, that I do not know what to do with myself. These girls have no Music, but Scotch Airs, no Drawings but Scotch Mountains, and no Books but Scotch Poems—And I hate everything Scotch. In general I can spend half the Day at my toilett with a great deal of pleasure, but why should I dress here, since there is not a creature in the House whom I have any wish to please.—. I have just had a conversation with my Brother in which he has greatly offended me, and which as I have nothing more entertaining to send you I will give you the particulars of. You must know that I have for these 4 or 5 Days past strongly suspected William of entertaining a partiality to my eldest Daughter. I own indeed that had *I* been inclined to fall in love with any woman, I should not have made choice of Matilda Lesley for the object of my passion; for there is nothing I hate so much as a tall Woman: but however there is no accounting for some men's taste and as William is himself nearly six feet high, it is not wonderful that he should be partial to that height. Now as I have a very great Affection for my Brother and should be extremely sorry to see him unhappy, which I suppose he means to be if he cannot marry Matilda, as moreover I know that his Circumstances will not allow him to marry any one without a fortune, and that Matilda's is entirely dependant on her Father, who will neither have his own inclination, nor my permission to give her anything at present, I thought it would be doing a good-natured action by my Brother to let him know as much, in order that he might choose for himself, whether to conquer his passion, or Love and Despair. Accordingly finding myself this Morning alone with him in one of the horrid rooms of this Castle, I opened the cause to him in the following Manner.

"Well my dear William what do you think of these girls? for my part, I do not find them so plain as I expected; but perhaps you may think me partial to the Daughters of my Husband and perhaps you are right—They are indeed so very like Sir George that it is natural to think. ." . . . .

"My Dear Susan (cried he in a tone of the greatest amazement) You do not really think they bear the least resemblance to their Father! He is so very plain!—but I beg your pardon—I had entirely forgotten to whom I was speaking—"

"Oh! pray dont mind me; (replied I) every one knows Sir George is horribly ugly, and I assure you I always thought him a fright."

"You surprise me extremely (answered William) by what you say both with respect to Sir George and his daughters. You cannot think your Husband so deficient in personal Charms as you speak of, nor can you surely see any resemblance between him and the Miss Lesleys who are in my opinion perfectly unlike him & perfectly Handsome."

"If that is your opinion with regard to the Girls it certainly is no proof of their Fathers beauty, for if they are perfectly unlike him and very handsome at the same time, it is natural to suppose that he is very plain."

"By no means, (said he) for what may be pretty in a Woman, may be very unpleasing in a Man."

"But you yourself (replied I) but a few Minutes ago allowed him to be very plain."

"Men are no Judges of Beauty in their own Sex." (said he)

"Neither Men nor Women can think Sir George tolerable."

"Well, well, (said he) we will not dispute about *his* Beauty, but your opinion of his *Daughters* is surely very singular, for if I understood you right, you said you did not find them so plain as you expected to do."!

"Why, do *you* find them plainer then?" (said I).

"I can scarcely beleive you to be serious (returned he) when you speak of their persons in so extroidinary a Manner. Do not you think the Miss Lesleys are two very handsome young Women?"

"Lord! No! (cried I) I think them terribly plain!"

"Plain! (replied He) My dear Susan, you cannot really think so! why what single Feature in the face of either of them, can you possible find fault with?"

"Oh! trust me for that; (replied I). Come I will begin with the eldest—with Matilda. Shall I, William? (I looked as cunning as I could when I said it, in order to shame him.)

"They are so much alike (said he) that I should suppose the faults of one, would be the faults of both."

"Well, then, in the first place, they are both so horribly tall!"

"They are *taller* than you are indeed." (said he with a saucy smile).

"Nay, (said I); I know nothing of that."

"Well, but (he continued) tho' they may be above the common size, their figures are perfectly elegant; and as to their faces, their Eyes are beautifull—."

"I can never think such tremendous knock-me-down figures in the least degree elegant, and as for their eyes, they are so tall that I never could strain my neck enough to look at them."

"Nay, (replied he), I know not whether you may not be in the right in not attempting it, for perhaps they might dazzle you with their Lustre."

"Oh! Certainly." (said I, with the greatest Complacency, for I assure you my dearest Charlotte I was not in the least offended tho' by what followed, one would suppose that William was conscious of having given me just cause to be so, for coming up to me and taking my hand, he said) "You must not look so grave Susan; you will make me fear I have offended you!"

"Offended me! Dear Brother, how came such a thought in your head! (returned I) No really! I assure you that I am not in the least surprised at your being so warm an advocate for the Beauty of these girls"—

"Well, but (interrupted William) remember that we have not yet concluded our dispute concerning them. What fault do you find with their complexion?"

"They are so horribly pale."

"They always have a little colour, and after any exercise it is considerably heightened."

"Yes, but if there should ever happen to be any rain in this part of the world, they will never be able to raise more than their common stock—except indeed they amuse themselves with running up & Down these horrid Galleries and Antichambers—"

"Well, (replied my Brother in a tone of vexation, & glancing an impertinent Look at me) if they *have* but little colour, at least, it is all their own."

This was too much my dear Charlotte, for I am certain that he had the impudence by that look, of pretending to suspect the reality of mine. But you I am sure will indicate my character whenever you may hear it so cruelly aspersed, for you can witness how often I have protested against wearing Rouge, and how much I always told you I dislike it. And I assure you that my opinions are still the same.—. Well, not bearing to be so suspected by my Brother, I left the room immediately, and have ever since been in my own Dressing-room writing to you. What a long Letter have I made of it!

L.F.—4

But you must not expect to receive such from me when I get to Town; for it is only at Lesley castle, that one has time to write even to a Charlotte Lutterell.—. I was so much vexed by William's Glance, that I could not summon Patience enough, to stay & give him that Advice respecting his Attachment to Matilda which had first induced me from pure Love to him to begin the conversation; and I am now so thoroughly convinced by it, of his violent passion for her, that I am certain he would never hear reason on the Subject, and I shall therefore give myself no more trouble either about him or his favourite. Adeiu my dear Girl—

Yrs Affectionately Susan L.

Letter the seventh
From Miss C. Lutterell to Miss M.
Lesley

Bristol

the 27th of March

I have received Letters from You & your Mother-in-Law within this week which have greatly entertained me, as I find by them that you are both downright jealous of each others Beauty. It is very odd that two pretty Women tho' actually Mother & Daughter cannot be in the same House without falling out about their faces. Do be convinced that you are both perfectly handsome and say no more of the Matter. I suppose this Letter must be directed to Portman Square where probably (great as is your affection for Lesley Castle) you will not be sorry to find yourself. In spite of all that People may say about Green fields and the Country I was always of the opinion that London and its Amusements must be very agreable for a while, and should be very happy could my Mother's income allow her to jockey us into its Public-places, during Winter. I always longed particularly to go to Vauxhall, to see whether the cold Beef there is cut so thin as

it is reported, for I have a sly suspicion that few people
understand the art of cutting a slice of cold Beef so well
as I do: nay it would be hard if I did not know something
of the Matter, for it was a part of my Education that I
took by far the most pains with. Mama always found me
her best Scholar, tho' when Papa was alive Eloisa was
his. Never to be sure were there two more different Dis-
positions in the World. We both loved Reading. *She* preferred Histories, & *I* Receipts. She loved drawing Pic-
tures, and I drawing Pullets. No one could sing a better
Song than She, and no one make a better Pye than I.—
And so it has always continued since we have been no
longer Children. The only difference is that all disputes
on the superior excellence of our Employments *then* so
frequent are now no more. We have for many years
entered into an agreement always to admire each other's
works; I never fail listening to *her* Music, & she is as
constant in eating *my* pies. Such at least was the case till
Henry Hervey made his appearance in Sussex. Before the
arrival of his Aunt in our neighbourhood where she
established herself you know about a twelvemonth ago,
his visits to her had been at stated times, and of equal &
settled Duration; but on her removal to the Hall which
is within a walk from our House, they became both more
frequent & longer. This as you may suppose could not
be pleasing to Mrs Diana who is a professed Enemy to
everything which is not directed by Decorum and For-
mality, or which bears the least resemblance to Ease and
Good-breeding. Nay so great was her aversion to her
Nephews behaviour that I have often heard her give
such hints of it before his face that had not Henry at
such times been engaged in conversation with Eloisa,
they must have caught his Attention and have very much
distressed him. The alteration in my Sisters behaviour
which I have before hinted at, now took place. The
Agreement we had entered into of admiring each others
productions she no longer seemed to regard & tho' I

constantly applauded even every Country-dance, She
play'd, yet not even a pidgeon-pye of my making could
obtain from her a single word of approbation. This was
certainly enough to put any one in a Passion; however,
I was as cool as a Cream-cheese and having formed my
plan & concerted a scheme of Revenge, I was determined
to let her have her own way & not even to make her a
single reproach. My Scheme was to treat her as she
treated me, and tho' she might even draw my own Picture or play Malbrook (which is the only tune I ever
really li'·e) not to say so much as "Thank you Eloisa;"
tho' I had for many years constantly hollowed whenever
she played, *Bravo, Bravissimo, Encora, Da Capo, allegretto,
con expressione,* and *Poco presto* with many other such out-
landish words, all of them as Eloisa told me expressive
of my Admiration; and so indeed I suppose they are, as
I see some of them in every Page of every Music book,
being the Sentiments I imagine of the Composer.

I executed my Plan with great Punctuality; I can not
say success, for Alas! my silence while she played seemed
not in the least to displease her; on the contrary she
actually said to me one day "Well Charlotte, I am very
glad to find that you have at last left off that ridiculous
custom of applauding my Execution in the Harpsichord
till you made *my* head ake, & yourself hoarse. I feel very
much obliged to you for keeping your Admiration to
yourself." I never shall forget the very witty answer I
made to this speech. "Eloisa (said I) I beg you would be
quite at your Ease with respect to all such fears in future,
for be assured that I shall always keep my Admiration
to myself, & my own pursuits & never extend it to yours."
This was the only very severe thing I ever said in my
Life; not but that I have often felt myself extremely
satirical but it was the only time I ever made my feelings
public.

I suppose there never were two young people who had
a greater affection for each other than Henry & Eloisa;

no, the Love of your Brother for Miss Burton could not
be so strong tho' it might be more violent. You may
imagine therefore how provoked my Sister must have
been to have him play her such a trick. Poor Girl! she
still laments his Death with undiminushed Constancy,
notwithstanding he has been dead more than six weeks;
but some people mind such things more than others.
The ill state of Health into which his Loss has thrown
her makes her so weak, & so unable to support the least
exertion, that she has been in tears all this Morning
merely from having taken Leave of Mrs Marlowe who
with Her husband, Brother and Child are to leave Bristol
this Morning. I am sorry to have them go because they
are the only family with whom we have here any acquaintance, but I never thought of crying; to be sure Eloisa &
Mrs Marlowe have always been more together than
with me, and have therefore contracted a kind of affection for each other, which does not make Tears so inex-
cusable in them as they would be in me. The Marlowes
are going to Town; Cleveland accompanies them; as
neither Eloisa nor I could catch him I hope you or
Matilda may have better Luck. I know not when we
shall leave Bristol, Eloisa's Spirits are so low that she is
very averse to moving, and yet is certainly by no means
mended by her residence here. A week or two will I hope
determine our Measures—in the mean time believe me
&c—&c—Charlotte Lutterell

Letter the Eighth
Miss Lutterell to Mrs Marlowe.

Bristol

April 4th

I feel myself greatly obliged to you my dear Emma for
such a mark of your affection as I flatter myself was conveyed in the proposal you made me of our Correspond-
ing; I assure you that it will be a great relief to me to

write to you and as long as my Health & Spirits will
allow me, you will find me a very constant Correspon-
dent; I will not say an entertaining one, for you know
my situation sufficiently not to be ignorant that in me
Mirth would be improper & I know my own Heart too
well not to be sensible that it would be unnatural. You
must not expect News for we see no one with whom we
are in the least acquainted, or in whose proceedings we
have any Interest. You must not expect Scandal for by
the same rule we are equally debarred either from hearing or inventing it.—You must expect from me nothing
but the melancholy effusions of a broken Heart which is
ever reverting to the Happiness it once enjoyed and
which ill supports its present wretchedness. The Possi-
bility of being able to write, to speak, to you, of my lost
Henry will be a Luxury to me, & your Goodness will not
I know refuse to read what it will so much releive my
Heart to write. I once thought that to have what is in
general called a Freind (I mean one of my own Sex to
whom I might speak with less reserve than to any other
person) independant of my Sister would never be an object of my wishes, but how much was I mistaken! Charlotte is too much engrossed by two confidential Corre-
spondents of that sort, to supply the place of one to me,
& I hope you will not think me girlishly romantic, when
I say that to have some kind and compassionate Freind
who might listen to my Sorrows without endeavouring
to console me was what I had for some time wished for,
when our acquaintance with you, the intimacy which
followed it & the particular affectionate Attention you
paid me almost from the first, caused me to entertain the
flattering Idea of those attentions being improved on a
closer acquaintance into a Freindship which, if you were
what my wishes formed you would be the greatest Happiness I could be capable of enjoying. To find that such
Hopes are realised is a satisfaction indeed, a satisfaction
which is now almost the only one I can ever experience.

—I feel myself so languid that I am sure were you with
me you would oblige me to leave off writing, & I cannot
give you a greater proof of my Affection for you than by
acting as I know you would wish me to do, whether Ab-
sent or Present. I am my dear Emmas sincere freind.

E.L.

Letter the Ninth
Mrs Marlowe to Miss Lutterell

Grosvenor Street,

April 10th

Need I say my dear Eloisa how wellcome your Letter
was to me? I cannot give a greater proof of the pleasure
I received from it, or of the Desire I feel that our Correspondence may be regular & frequent than by setting
you so good an example as I now do in answering it before the end of the week—. But do not imagine that I
claim any merit in being so punctual; on the contrary I
assure you, that it is a far greater Gratification to me to
write to you, than to spend the Evening either at a Concert or a Ball. Mr Marlowe is so desirous of my appearing
at some of the Public places every evening that I do not
like to refuse him, but at the same time so much wish to
remain at Home, that independant of the Pleasure I experience in devoting any portion of my Time to my Dear
Eloisa, yet the Liberty I claim from having a Letter to
write of spending an Evening at home with my little
Boy, You know me well enough to be sensible, will of
itself be a sufficient Inducement (if one is necessary) to
my maintaining with Pleasure a Correspondence with
you. As to the Subjects of your Letters to me, whether
Grave or Merry, if they concern you they must be equally
interesting to me; Not but that I think the Melancholy
Indulgence of your own Sorrows by repeating them &
dwelling on them to me, will only encourage and in-
crease them, and that it will be more prudent in you to

avoid so sad a subject; but yet knowing as I do what a
soothing & Melancholy Pleasure it must afford you, I
cannot prevail on myself to deny you so great an Indulgence, and will only insist on your not expecting me to
encourage you in it, by my own Letters; on the contrary
I intend to fill them with such lively Wit and enlivening
Humour as shall even provoke a Smile in the sweet but
sorrowfull Countenance of my Eloisa.

In the first place you are to learn that I have met your
Sisters three freinds Lady Lesley and her Daughters,
twice in Public since I have been here. I know you will
be impatient to hear my opinion of the Beauty of three
Ladies of whom You have heard so much. Now, as you
are too ill & too unhappy to be vain, I think I may ven-
ture to inform you that I like none of their faces so well
as I do your own. Yet they are all handsome—Lady
Lesley indeed I have seen before; her Daughters I beleive
would in general be said to have a finer face than her
Ladyship, and Yet what with the charms of a Blooming
Complexion, a little Affectation and a great deal of
Small-talk, (in each of which She is superior to the
Young Ladies) she will I dare say gain herself as many
Admirers as the more regular features of Matilda, &
Margaret. I am sure you will agree with me in saying
that they can none of them be of a proper size for real
Beauty, when you know that two of them are taller &
the other shorter than ourselves. In spite of this Defect
(or rather by reason of it) there is something very noble
& majestic in the figures of the Miss Lesleys, and something agreably Lively in the Appearance of their pretty
little Mother-in-law. But tho' one may be majestic & the
other Lively, yet the faces of neither possess that Bewitching Sweetness of my Eloisas, which her present Languor
is so far from diminishing. What would my Husband
and Brother say of us, if they knew all the fine things I
have been saying to you in this Letter. It is very hard
that a pretty Woman is never to be told she is so by any

one of her own Sex, without that person's being suspected
to be either her determined Enemy, or her professed
Toad-eater. How much more amiable are women in that
particular! one man may say forty civil things to another
without our supposing that he is ever paid for it, and
provided he does his Duty by our Sex, we care not how
Polite he is to his own.

Mrs Lutterell will be so good as to accept my Compliments, Charlotte, my Love, and Eloisa the best wishes
for the recovery of her Health & Spirits that can be
offered by her Affectionate Freind

E. Marlowe

I am afraid this Letter will be but a poor Specimen of
my Powers in the Witty Way; and your opinion of them
will not be greatly increased when I assure you that I
have been as entertaining as I possibly could—.

Letter the Tenth
From Miss Margaret Lesley to Miss
Charlotte Lutterell.

Portman Square
April 13th

My dear Charlotte
We left Lesley-Castle on the 28th of Last Month, and
arrived Safely in London after a Journey of seven Days;
I had the pleasure of finding your Letter here waiting
my Arrival, for which you have my grateful Thanks. Ah!
my dear Freind I every day more regret the serene and
tranquil Pleasures of the Castle we have left, in exchange
for the uncertain & unequal Amusements of this vaunted
City. Not that I will pretend to assert that these uncertain and unequal Amusements are in the least Degree
unpleasing to me; on the contrary I enjoy them extremely and should enjoy them even more, were I not certain that every appearance I make in Public but rivetts
the Chains of those unhappy Beings whose Passion it is

impossible not to pity, tho' it is out of my power to return. In short my dear Charlotte it is my sensibility for the sufferings of so many amiable Young Men, my Dislike of the extreme Admiration I meet with, and my Aversion to being so celebrated both in Public, in Private, in Papers, & in Printshops, that are the reasons why I cannot more fully enjoy, the Amusements so various and pleasing of London. How often have I wished that I possessed as little personal Beauty as you do; that my figure were as inelegant; my face as unlovely; and my Appearance as unpleasing as yours! But ah! what little chance is there of so desirable an Event; I have had the Small-pox, and must therefore submit to my unhappy fate.

I am now going to intrust you my dear Charlotte with a secret which has long disturbed the tranquillity of my days, and which is of a kind to require the most inviolable Secrecy from you. Last Monday se'night Matilda & I accompanied Lady Lesley to a Rout at the Honourable Mrs Kickabout's; we were escorted by Mr Fitzgerald who is a very amiable Young Man in the main, tho' perhaps a little singular in his Taste—He is in love with Matilda—We had scarcely paid our Compliments to the Lady of the House and curtseyed to half a Score different people when my Attention was attracted by the appearance of a Young Man the most lovely of his Sex, who at that moment entered the Room with another Gentleman & Lady. From the first moment I beheld him, I was certain that on him depended the future Happiness of my Life. Imagine my surprise when he was introduced to me by the name of Cleveland—I instantly recognised him as the Brother of Mrs Marlowe, and the acquaintance of my Charlotte at Bristol. Mr and Mrs M. were the gentleman & Lady who accompanied him. (You do not think Mrs Marlowe handsome?) The elegant address of Mr Cleveland, his polished Manners and Delightful Bow, at once confirmed my attachment. He did not speak; but I can imagine every thing he would have

said, had he opened his Mouth. I can picture to myself
the cultivated Understanding, the Noble Sentiments, &
elegant Language which would have shone so conspicuous in the conversation of Mr Cleveland. The ap-
proach of Sir James Gower (one of my too numerous
Admirers) prevented the Discovery of any such Powers,
by putting an end to a conversation we had never commenced, and by attracting my attention to himself. But
oh! how inferior are the accomplishments of Sir James
to those of his so greatly envied Rival! Sir James is one
of the most frequent of our Visitors, & is almost always
of our Parties. We have since often met Mr & Mrs Marlowe but no Cleveland—he is always engaged some where
else. Mrs Marlowe fatigues me to Death every time I see
her by her tiresome conversations about You & Eloisa.
She is so Stupid! I live in the hope of seeing her irrisist-
able Brother to night, as we are going to Lady Flambeau's, who is I know intimate with the Marlowes. Our
party will be Lady Lesley, Matilda, Fitzgerald, Sir James
Gower, & myself. We see little of Sir George, who is almost always at the Gaming-table. Ah! my poor Fortune,
where art thou by this time? We see more of Lady L.
who always makes her appearance (highly rouged) at
Dinner-time. Alas! what Delightful Jewels will she be
decked in this evening at Lady Flambeau's!; Yet I wonder how she can herself delight in wearing them; surely
she must be sensible of the ridiculous impropriety of load-
ing her little diminutive figure with such superfluous
ornaments; is it possible that she can not know how
greatly superior an elegant simplicity is to the most
studied apparel? Would she but present them to Matilda
& me, how greatly should we be obliged to her. How
becoming would Diamonds be on our fine majestic
figures! And how surprising it is that such an Idea should
never have occurred to *her*. I am sure if I have reflected
in this Manner once, I have fifty times. Whenever I see
Lady Lesley dressed in them such reflections immediately

come across me. My own Mother's Jewels too! But I will say no more on so melancholy a Subject—Let me entertain you with something more pleasing—Matilda had a letter this Morning from Lesley, by which we have the pleasure of finding he is at Naples has turned Roman-catholic, obtained one of the Pope's Bulls for annulling his 1st Marriage and had since actually married a Neapolitan Lady of great Rank & Fortune. He tells us moreover that much the same sort of affair has befallen his first wife the worthless Louisa who is likewise at Naples has turned Roman-catholic, and is soon to be married to a Neapolitan Nobleman of great & Distinguished Merit. He says, that they are at present very good Freinds, have quite forgiven all past errors and intend in future to be very good Neighbours. He invites Matilda & me to pay him a visit in Italy and to bring him his little Louisa whom both her Mother, Step-Mother, and himself are equally desirous of beholding. As to our accepting his invitation, it is at present very uncertain; Lady Lesley advises us to go without loss of time; Fitzgerald offers to escort us there, but Matilda has some doubts of the Propriety of such a Scheme—She owns it would be very agreable. I am certain she likes the Fellow. My Father desires us not to be in a hurry, as perhaps if we wait a few months both he & Lady Lesley will do themselves the pleasure of attending us. Lady Lesley says no, that nothing will ever tempt her to forego the Amusements of Brighthelmstone for a Journey to Italy merely to see our Brother. "No (says the disagreable woman) I have once in my life been fool enough to travel I dont know how many hundred Miles to see two of the Family, and I found it did not answer, so Deuce take me, if ever I am so foolish again." So says her Ladyship, but Sir George still perseveres in saying that perhaps in a Month or two, they may accompany us.

Adeiu my Dear Charlotte
Yr faithful Margaret Lesley

THE
HISTORY
OF
ENGLAND

FROM THE REIGN OF HENRY THE 4TH
TO THE DEATH OF CHARLES THE IST.

By a partial, prejudiced, & ignorant Historian. To Miss
Austen eldest daughter of the Revd George Austen, this
Work is inscribed with all due respect by

The Author

N.B. There will be very few Dates in this History.

Henry the 4th

Henry the 4th ascended the throne of England much to his own satisfaction in the year 1399, after having prevailed on his cousin & predecessor Richard the 2d, to resign it to him, & to retire for the rest of his Life to Pomfret Castle, where he happened to be murdered. It is to be supposed that Henry was married, since he had certainly four sons, but it is not in my power to inform the Reader who was his Wife. Be this as it may, he did not live for ever, but falling ill, his son the Prince of Wales came and took away the crown; whereupon the King made a long speech, for which I must refer the Reader to Shakespear's Plays, & the Prince made a still longer. Things being thus settled between them the King died, & was succeeded by his son Henry who had previously beat Sir William Gascoigne.

Henry the 5th

This Prince after he succeeded to the throne grew quite reformed & Amiable, forsaking all his dissipated Companions, & never thrashing Sir William again. During his reign, Lord Cobham was burnt alive, but I forget what for. His Majesty then turned his thoughts to France, where he went & fought the famous Battle of Agincourt. He afterwards married the King's daughter Catherine, a very agreable Woman by Shakespear's account. In spite of all this however he died, and was succeeded by his son Henry.

Henry the 6th

I cannot say much for this Monarch's Sense—Nor would I if I could, for he was a Lancastrian. I suppose you know all about the Wars between him & The Duke

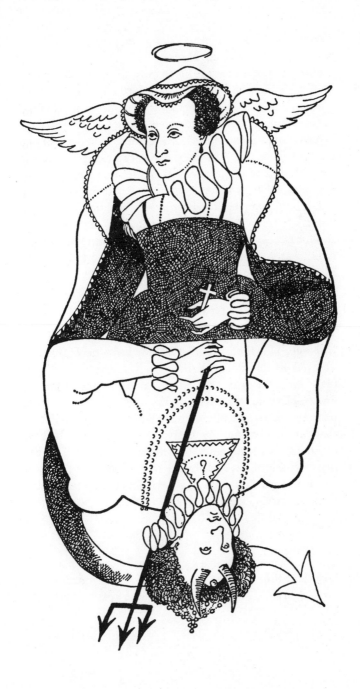

of York who was of the right side; If you do not, you had better read some other History, for I shall not be very diffuse in this, meaning by it only to vent my Spleen *against*, & shew my Hatred *to* all those people whose parties or principles do not suit with mine, & not to give information. This King married Margaret of Anjou, a Woman whose distresses & Misfortunes were so great as almost to make me who hate her, pity her. It was in this reign that Joan of Arc lived & made such a *row* among the English. They should not have burnt her—but they did. There were several Battles between the Yorkists & Lancastrians, in which the former (as they ought) usually conquered. At length they were entirely over come; The King was murdered—The Queen was sent home—& Edward the 4th Ascended the Throne.

Edward the 4th

This Monarch was famous only for his Beauty & his Courage, of which the Picture we have here given of him, & his undaunted Behaviour in marrying one Woman while he was engaged to another, are sufficient proofs. His wife was Elizabeth Woodville, a Widow, who, poor Woman!, was afterwards confined in a Convent by that Monster of Iniquity & Avarice Henry the 7th. One of Edward's Mistresses was Jane Shore, who has had a play written about her, but it is a tragedy & therefore not worth reading. Having performed all these noble actions, his Majesty died, & was succeeded by his Son.

Edward the 5th

This unfortunate Prince lived so little a while that no body had time to draw his picture. He was murdered by his Uncle's Contrivance, whose name was Richard the 3d.

Richard the 3rd

The Character of this Prince has been in general very severely treated by Historians, but as he was *York*, I am rather inclined to suppose him a very respectable Man. It has indeed been confidently asserted that he killed his two Nephews & his Wife, but it has also been declared that he did *not* kill his two Nephews, which I am inclined to beleive true; & if this is the case, it may also be affirmed that he did not kill his Wife, for if Perkin Warbeck was really the Duke of York, why might not Lambert Simnel be the Widow of Richard. Whether innocent or guilty, he did not reign long in peace, for Henry Tudor E. of Richmond as great a Villain as ever lived, made a great fuss about getting the Crown & having killed the King at the battle of Bosworth, he succeeded to it.

Henry the 7th

This Monarch soon after his accession married the Princess Elizabeth of York, by which alliance he plainly proved that he thought his own right inferior to hers, tho' he pretended to the contrary. By this Marriage he had two sons & two daughters, the elder of which daughters was married to the King of Scotland & had the happiness of being grand-mother to one of the first Characters in the World. But of *her*, I shall have occasion to speak more at large in future. The Youngest, Mary, married first the King of France & secondly the D. of Suffolk, by whom she had one daughter, afterwards the Mother of Lady Jane Grey, who tho' inferior to her lovely Cousin the Queen of Scots, was yet an amiable young woman and famous for reading Greek while other people were hunting. It was in the reign of Henry the 7th that Perkin Warbeck & Lambert Simnel before mentioned made their appearance, the former of whom was set in the Stocks, took shelter in Beaulieu Abbey, & was beheaded with the Earl of Warwick, & the latter was taken

into the King's Kitchen. His Majesty died, & was succeeded by his son Henry whose only merit was his not
being *quite* so bad as his daughter Elizabeth.

Henry the 8th

It would be an affront to my Readers were I to suppose
that they were not as well acquainted with the particulars
of this King's reign as I am myself. It will therefore be
saving *them* the task of reading again what they have
read before, & *myself* the trouble of writing what I do
not perfectly recollect, by giving only a slight sketch of
the principal Events which marked his reign. Among
these may be ranked Cardinal Wolsey's telling the father
Abbott of Leicester Abbey that "he was come to lay his
bones among them", the reformation in Religion, & the
King's riding through the Streets of London with Anna
Bullen. It is however but Justice, & my Duty to declare
that this amiable Woman was entirely innocent of the
Crimes with which she was accused, of which her Beauty,
her Elegance, & her Sprightliness were sufficient proofs,
not to mention her solemn protestations of Innocence,
the weakness of the Charges against her, and the king's
Character; all of which add some confirmation, tho' perhaps but slight ones when in comparison with those before alledged in her favour. Tho' I do not profess giving
many dates, yet as I think it proper to give some & shall
of course make choice of those which it is most necessary
for the Reader to know, I think it right to inform him
that her letter to the King was dated on the 6th of May.
The Crimes & Cruelties of this Prince, were too numerous to be mentioned, (as this history I trust has fully
shown;) & nothing can be said in his vindication, but
that his abolishing Religious Houses & leaving them to
the ruinous depredations of time has been of infinite use
to the landscape of England in general, which probably
was a principal motive for his doing it, since otherwise

why should a Man who was of no Religion himself be at so much trouble to abolish one which had for Ages been established in the Kingdom. His Majesty's 5th wife was the Duke of Norfolk's Neice who, tho' universally acquitted of the crimes for which she was beheaded, has been by many people supposed to have led an abandoned Life before her Marriage—of this however I have many doubts, since she was a relation of that noble Duke of Norfolk who was so warm in the Queen of Scotland's cause, & who at last fell a victim to it. The king's last wife contrived to survive him, but with difficulty effected it. He was succeeded by his only son Edward.

Edward the 6th

As this prince was only nine years old at the time of his Father's death, he was considered by many people as too young to govern, & the late King happening to be of the same opinion, his mother's Brother the Duke of Somerset was chosen Protector of the realm during his minority. This Man was on the whole of a very amiable Character, & is somewhat of a favourite with me, tho' I would by no means pretend to affirm that he was equal to those first of Men Robert Earl of Essex, Delamere, or Gilpin. He was beheaded, of which he might with reason have been proud, had he known that such was the death of Mary Queen of Scotland; but as it was impossible that He should be conscious of what had never happened, it does not appear that he felt particularly delighted with the manner of it. After his decease the Duke of Northumberland had the care of the King & the Kingdom, & performed his trust of both so well that the King died & the Kingdom was left to his daughter in law the Lady Jane Grey, who had been already mentioned as reading Greek. Whether she really understood that language or whether such a Study proceeded only from an excess of vanity for which I beleive she was always rather remark-

able, is uncertain. Whatever might be the cause, she pre-
served the same appearance of knowledge, & contempt
of what was generally esteemed pleasure, during the
whole of her Life, for she declared herself displeased with
being appointed Queen, and while conducting to the
Scaffold, she wrote a Sentence in Latin & another in
Greek on seeing the dead Body of her Husband accidentally passing that way.

Mary

This Woman had the good luck of being advanced to the
throne of England, inspite of the superior pretensions,
Merit, & *Beauty* of her Cousins Mary Queen of Scotland
& Jane Grey. Nor can I pity the Kingdom for the misfortunes they experienced during her Reign, since they
fully deserved them, for having allowed her to succeed
her Brother—which was a double peice of folly, since
they might have foreseen that as she died without Children, she would be succeeded by that disgrace to human-
ity, that pest of society, Elizabeth. Many were the people
who fell Martyrs to the Protestant Religion during her
reign; I suppose not fewer than a dozen. She married
Philip King of Spain who in her Sister's reign was famous
for building Armadas. She died with out issue, &
then the dreadful moment came in which the destroyer
of all comfort, the deceitful Betrayer of trust reposed
in her, & the Murderess of her Cousin succeeded to the
Throne.

Elizabeth

It was the peculiar Misfortune of this Woman to have
bad Ministers—Since wicked as she herself was, she could
not have committed such extensive mischief, had not
these vile & abandoned men connived at, & encouraged
her in her crimes. I know that it has by many people
been asserted & beleived that Lord Burleigh, Sir Francis
Walsingham, & the rest of those who filled the cheif

offices of State were deserving, experienced, & able Ministers. But oh! how blinded such Writers & such Readers must be to true Merit, to Merit despised, neglected & defamed, if they can persist in such opinions when they reflect that these Men, these boasted Men were such Scandals to their Country & their Sex as to allow & assist their Queen in confining for the space of nineteen years, a *Woman* who if the claims of Relationship & Merit were no avail, yet as a Queen & as one who condescended to place confidence in her, had every reason to expect Assistance & Protection; and at length in allowing Elizabeth to bring this amiable Woman to an untimely, unmerited, and scandalous Death. Can any one if he reflects but for a moment on this blot, this everlasting blot upon their Understanding & their Character, allow any praise to Lord Burleigh or Sir Francis Walsingham? Oh! what must this bewitching Princess whose only freind was then the Duke of Norfolk, and who only ones are now Mr Whitaker, Mrs Lefroy, Mrs Knight & myself, who was abandoned by her son, confined by her Cousin, Abused, reproached & villified by all, what must not her most noble mind have suffered when informed that Elizabeth had given orders for her Death! Yet she bore it with a most unshaken fortitude; firm in her Mind; Constant in her Religion; & prepared herself to meet the cruel fate to which she was doomed, with a magnanimity that could alone proceed from conscious Innocence. And yet could you Reader have beleived it possible that some hardened & zealous Protestants have even abused her for that Steadfastness in the Catholic Religion which reflected on her so much credit? But this is a striking proof of *their* narrow Souls & prejudiced Judgements who accuse her. She was executed in the Great Hall at Fortheringay Castle (sacred Place!) on Wednesday the 8th of February 1586—to the everlasting Reproach of Elizabeth, her Ministers, and of England in general. It may not be unnecessary before I entirely conclude my account of this ill-fated Queen, to observe that she had been accused of several crimes during the time of her reigning in Scotland, of which I now most seriously do assure my Reader that she was entirely innocent; having never been guilty of anything more than Imprudencies into which she was betrayed by the openness of her Heart, her Youth, & her Education. Having I trust by this assurance entirely done away every Suspicion & every doubt which might have arisen in the Reader's mind, from what other Historians have written of her, I shall proceed to mention the remaining Events that marked Elizabeth's reign. It was about this time that Sir Francis Drake the first English Navigator who sailed round the World, lived, to be the ornament of his Country & his profession. Yet great as he was, & justly celebrated as a Sailor, I cannot help foreseeing that he will be equalled in this or the next Century by one who tho' now but young, already promises to answer all the ardent & sanguine expectations of his Relations & Freinds, amongst whom I may class the amiable Lady to whom this work is dedicated, & my no less amiable Self.

Though of a different profession, and shining in a different Sphere of Life, yet equally conspicuous in the Character of an *Earl*, as Drake was in that of a *Sailor*, was Robert Devereux Lord Essex. This unfortunate young Man was not unlike in Character to that equally unfortunate one *Frederic Delamere*. The simile may be carried still farther, & Elizabeth the torment of Essex may be compared to the Emmeline of Delamere. It would be endless to recount the misfortunes of this noble & gallant Earl. It is sufficient to say that he was beheaded on the 25th of Febry, after having been Lord Leuitenant of Ireland, after having clapped his hand on his sword, and after performing many other services to his Country. Elizabeth did not long survive his loss, & died *so* miserable that were it not an injury to the memory of Mary I should pity her.

James the 1st

Though this King had some faults, among which & as the most principal, was his allowing his Mother's death, yet considered on the whole I cannot help liking him. He married Anne of Denmark, and had several Children; fortunately for him his eldest son Prince Henry died before his father or he might have experienced the evils which befell his unfortunate Brother.

As I am myself partial to the roman catholic religion, it is with infinite regret that I am obliged to blame the Behaviour of any Member of it; yet Truth being I think very excusable in an Historian, I am necessitated to say that in this reign the roman Catholics of England did not behave like Gentlemen to the protestants. Their Behaviour indeed to the Royal Family & both Houses of Parliament might justly be considered by them as very uncivil, and even Sir Henry Percy tho' certainly the best bred Man of the party, had none of that general politeness which is so universally pleasing, as his Attentions were entirely confined to Lord Mounteagle.

Sir Walter Raleigh flourished in this & the preceeding reign, & is by many people held in great veneration & respect—But as he was an enemy of the noble Essex, I have nothing to say in praise of him, & must refer all those who may wish to be acquainted with the particulars of his Life, to Mr Sheridan's play of the Critic, where they will find many interesting Anecdotes as well of him as of his freind Sir Christopher Hatton.—. His Majesty was of that amiable disposition which inclines to Freindships, & in such points was possessed of a keener penetration in Discovering Merit than many other people. I once heard an excellent Sharade on a Carpet, of which the subject I am now on reminds me, and as I think it may afford my Readers some Amusement to *find it out,* I shall here take the liberty of presenting it to them.

SHARADE

My first is what my second was to King James the 1st,
and you tread on my whole.

The principal favourites of his Majesty were Car, who
was afterwards created Earl of Somerset and whose name
may have some share in the above mentioned Sharade,
& George Villiers afterwards Duke of Buckingham. On
his Majesty's death he was succeeded by his son Charles.

Charles the 1st

This amiable Monarch seems born to have suffered Misfortunes equal to those of his lovely Grandmother; Misfortunes which he could not deserve since he was her de-
scendant. Never certainly was there before so many de-
testable Characters at one time in England as in this
period of its History; Never were amiable Men so scarce.
The number of them throughout the whole Kingdom
amounting only to *five*, besides the inhabitants of Oxford
who were always loyal to their King & faithful to his
interests. The names of this noble five who never forgot
the duty of the Subject, or swerved from their attachment to his Majesty, were as follows,—The King himself,
ever stedfast in his own support—Archbishop Laud, Earl
of Strafford, Viscount Faulkland & Duke of Ormond
who were scarcely less strenuous or zealous in the cause.
While the Villains of the time would make too long a
list to be written or read; I shall therefore content myself with mentioning the leaders of the Gang. Cromwell,
Fairfax, Hampden, & Pym may be considered as the
original Causers of all the disturbances Distresses & Civil
Wars in which England for many years was embroiled.
In this reign as well as in that of Elizabeth, I am obliged
in spite of my Attachment to the Scotch, to consider
them as equally guilty with the generality of the English,
since they dared to think differently from their Sovereign,
to forget the Adoration which as *Stuarts* it was their Duty

to pay them, to rebel against, dethrone & imprison the unfortunate Mary; to oppose, to deceive, and to sell the no less unfortunate Charles. The Events of this Monarch's reign are too numerous for my pen, and indeed the recital of any Events (except what I make myself) is uninteresting to me; my principal reason for undertaking the History of England being to prove the innocence of the Queen of Scotland, which I flatter myself with having effectually done, and to abuse Elizabeth, tho' I am rather fearful of having fallen short in the latter part of my Scheme.—. As therefore it is not my intention to give any particular account of the distresses into which this King was involved through the misconduct & Cruelty of his Parliament, I shall satisfy myself with vindicating him from the Reproach of Arbitrary & tyrannical Government with which he has often been Charged. This, I feel, is not difficult to be done, for with one argument I am certain of satisfying every sensible & well disposed person whose opinions have been properly guided by a good Education—& this Arguement is that he was a Stuart.

Finis

Saturday Nov: 26th 1791

~~~~~~

A
COLLECTION
OF
LETTERS

~~~~~~

To Miss Cooper

Cousin
Conscious of the Charming Character which in every
Country, & every Clime in Christendom is Cried, Con-
cerning you, with Caution & Care I Commend to your
Charitable Criticism this Clever Collection of Curious
Comments, which have been Carefully Culled, Collected
& Classed by your Comical Cousin

The Author.

Letter the first

From A Mother to her freind

My Children begin now to claim all my attention in a different Manner from that in which they have been used to receive it, as they are now arrived at that age when it is necessary for them in some measure to become conversant with the World. My Augusta is 17 & her Sister scarcely a twelvemonth younger. I flatter myself that their education has been such as will not disgrace their appearance in the World, & that *they* will not disgrace their Education I have every reason to beleive. Indeed they are sweet Girls—. Sensible yet unaffected— Accomplished yet Easy—. Lively yet Gentle—. As their progress in every thing they have learnt has been always the same, I am willing to forget the difference of age, and to introduce them together into Public. This very Evening is fixed on as their first entrée into life, as we are to drink tea with Mrs Cope & her Daughter. I am glad that we are to meet no one for my Girls sake, as it would be awkward for them to enter too wide a Circle on the very first day. But we shall proceed by degrees—. Tomorrow Mr Stanly's family will drink tea with us, and perhaps the Miss Phillips will meet them. On Tuesday we shall pay Morning-Visits—On Wednesday we are to dine at Westbrook. On Thursday we have Company at home. On Friday we are to be at a private concert at Sir John Wynne's—& on Saturday we expect Miss Dawson to call in the morning,—which will complete my Daughters Introduction into Life. How they will bear so much dissipation I cannot imagine; of their Spirits I have no fear, I only dread their health.

This mighty affair is now happily over, & my Girls *are out.* As the moment approached for our departure, you

can have no idea how the sweet Creatures trembled with
fear & expectation. Before the Carriage drove to the door,
I called them into my dressing-room, & as soon as they
were seated thus addressed them. "My dear Girls the
moment is now arrived when I am to reap the rewards
of all my Anxieties and Labours towards you during your
Education. You are this Evening to enter a World in
which you will meet with many wonderfull Things; Yet
let me warn you against suffering yourselves to be meanly
swayed by the Follies & Vices of others, for beleive me
my beloved Children that if you do—I shall be very
sorry for it." They both assured me that they would ever
remember my advice with Gratitude, & follow it with
Attention; That they were prepared to find a World full
of things to amaze & shock them: but that they trusted
their behaviour would never give me reason to repent
the Watchful Care with which I had presided over their
infancy & formed their Minds—. "With such expectations & such intentions (cried I) I can have nothing to
fear from you—& can chearfully conduct you to Mrs
Cope's without a fear of your being seduced by her Example or contaminated by her Follies. Come, then my
Children (added I) the Carriage is driving to the door,
& I will not a moment delay the happiness you are so
impatient to enjoy." When we arrived at Warleigh, poor
Augusta could hardly breathe, while Margaret was all
Life & Rapture. "The long-expected Moment is now
arrived (said she) and we shall soon be in the World."—
In a few Moments we were in Mrs Cope's parlour—,
where with her daughter she sat ready to receive us. I
observed with delight the impression my Children made
on them—. They were indeed two sweet, elegant-looking
Girls, & tho' somewhat abashed from the peculiarity of
their Situation, Yet there was an ease in their Manners
& Address which could not fail of pleasing—. Imagine
my dear Madam how delighted I must have been in beholding as I did, how attentively they observed every ob-

ject they saw, how disgusted with some Things, how en-
chanted with others, how astonished at all! On the whole
however they returned in raptures with the World, its
Inhabitants, & Manners.

Yrs Ever—A–F–.

Letter the second

From a Young lady crossed in Love to her freind—

Why should this last disappointment hang so heavily on
my Spirits? Why should I feel it more, why should it
wound me deeper than those I have experienced before?
Can it be that I have a greater affection for Willoughby
than I had for his amiable predecessors? Or is it that
our feelings become more acute from being often wounded? I must suppose my dear Belle that this is the Case,
since I am not conscious of being more sincerely attached
to Willoughby than I was to Neville, Fitzowen, or either
of the Crawfords, for all of whom I once felt the most
lasting affection that ever warmed a Woman's heart. Tell
me then dear Belle why I still sigh when I think of the
faithless Edward, or why I weep when I behold his Bride,
for too surely this is the case—. My Freinds are all
alarmed for me; They fear my declining health; they
lament my want of Spirits; they dread the effects of both.
In hopes of releiving my Melancholy, by directing my
thoughts to other objects, they have invited several of
their freinds to spend the Christmas with us. Lady Bridget Dashwood & her Sister-in-Law Miss Jane are expected
on Friday; & Colonel Seaton's family will be with us
next week. This is all most kindly meant by my Uncle
& Cousins; but what can the presence of a dozen indifferent people do to me, but weary & distress me—. I
will not finish my Letter till some of our Visitors are
arrived.

Friday Evening

Lady Bridget came this Morning, and with her, her
sweet Sister Miss Jane—. Although I have been acquainted with this charming Woman above fifteen years, Yet
I never before observed how lovely she is. She is now
about 35, & in spite of sickness, Sorrow and Time is more
blooming than I ever saw a Girl of 17. I was delighted
with her, the moment she entered the house, & she appeared equally pleased with me, attaching herself to me
during the remainder of the day. There is something so
sweet, so mild in her Countenance, that she seems more
than Mortal. Her Conversation is as bewitching as her
appearance—; I could not help telling her how much
she engaged my Admiration—. —"Oh! Miss Jane" (said
I)—and stopped from an inability at the moment of expressing myself as I could wish—"Oh! Miss Jane" (I repeated)—I could not think of words to suit my feelings
—She seemed waiting for my Speech—. I was confused
—distressed—. My thoughts were bewildered—and I
could only add "How do you do?" She saw & felt for
my embarrassment & with admirable presence of mind
relieved me from it by saying—"My dear Sophia be not
uneasy at having exposed Yourself—I will turn the Conversation without appearing to notice it." Oh! how I
loved her for her kindness! "Do you ride as much as you
used to do?" said she—. "I am advised to ride by my
Physician, We have delightful Rides round us, I have a
charming horse, am uncommonly fond of the Amusement," replied I quite recovered from my confusion, "&
in short I ride a great deal." "You are in the right my
Love," said She, Then repeating the following Line
which was an extempore & equally adapted to recom-
mend both Riding & Candour—

"Ride where you may, Be Candid where You can,"
She added, "*I* rode once, but it is many years ago"—
She spoke this in so Low & tremulous a Voice, that I
was silent—Struck with her Manner of Speaking I could

make no reply. "I have not ridden, continued she fixing her Eyes on my face, since I was married." I was never so surprised—"Married, Ma'am,!" I repeated. "You may well wear that look of astonishment, said she, since what I have said must appear improbable to you—Yet nothing is more true than that I once was married."

"Then why are you called Miss Jane?"

"I married, my Sophia without the consent or know-ledge of my father—the late Admiral Annesley. It was therefore necessary to keep the secret from him & from every one, till some fortunate opportunity might offer of revealing it—. Such an opportunity alas! was but too soon given in the death of my dear Capt Dashwood— Pardon these tears, continued Miss Jane wiping her Eyes, I owe them to my Husband's Memory, He fell my Sophia, while fighting for his Country in America after a most happy Union of seven years—. My Children, two sweet Boys & a Girl, who had constantly resided with my Father & me, passing with him & with every one as the Children of a Brother (tho' I had ever been an only child) had as yet been the Comforts of my Life. But no sooner had I lossed my Henry, than these sweet Creatures fell sick & died—. Conceive dear Sophia what my feelings must have been when as an Aunt I attended my Children to their early Grave—. My Father did not survive them many weeks—He died, poor Good old Man, happily ig-norant to his last hour of my Marriage."

"But did you not own it, & assume his name at your husband's death?"

"No; I could not bring myself to do it; more especially when in my Children, I lost all inducement for doing it. Lady Bridget, and Yourself are the only persons who are in the knowledge of my having ever been either Wife or Mother. As I could not prevail on myself to take the name of Dashwood (a name which after my Henry's death I could never hear without emotion) and as I was conscious of having no right to that of Annesley, I dropt all thoughts

of either, & have made it a point of bearing only my
Christian one since my Father's death." She paused—
"Oh! my dear Miss Jane (said I) how infinitely am I
obliged to you for so entertaining a Story! You cannot
think how it has diverted me! But have you quite done?"

"I have only to add my dear Sophia, that my Henry's
elder Brother dieing about the same time, Lady Bridget
became a Widow like myself, and as we had always loved
each other in idea from the high Character in which we
had ever been spoken of, though we had never met, we
determined to live together. We wrote to one another on
the same subject by the same post, so exactly did our
feelings & our Actions coincide: We both eagerly em-
braced the proposals we gave & received of becoming
one family, and have from that time lived together in the
greatest affection."

"And is this all?" said I, "I hope you have not done."

"Indeed I have; and did you ever hear a Story more
pathetic?"

"I never did—and it is for that reason it pleases me so
much, for when one is unhappy nothing is so delightful
to one's sensations as to hear of equal Misery."

"Ah! but my Sophia why *are you* unhappy?"

"Have you not heard Madam of Willoughby's Marriage?" "But my Love why lament *his* perfidy, when you
bore so well that of many young Men before?" "Ah!
Madam, I was used to it then, but when Willoughby
broke his Engagements I had not been dissapointed for
half a year." "Poor Girl!" said Miss Jane.

Letter the third

From A young Lady in distress'd Circum-
stances to her freind.

A few days ago I was at a private Ball given by Mr Ash-
burnham. As my Mother never goes out she entrusted
me to the care of Lady Greville who did me the honour

of calling for me in her way & of allowing me to sit forwards, which is a favour about which I am very indifferent especially as I know it is considered as confering
a great obligation on me. "So Miss Maria (said her Ladyship as she saw me advancing to the door of the Carriage)
you seem very smart tonight—*My* poor Girls will appear
quite to disadvantage by *you*. I only hope your Mother
may not have distressed herself to set *you* off. Have you
got a new Gown on?"

"Yes Ma'am," replied I with as much indifference as
I could assume.

"Aye, and a fine one too I think—(feeling it, as by
her permission I seated myself by her) I dare say it is all
very smart—But I must own, for you know I always
speak my mind, that I think it was quite a needless peice
of expence—Why could not you have worn your old
striped one? It is not my way to find fault with people
because they are poor, for I always think that they are
more to be despised & pitied than blamed for it, especially if they cannot help it, but at the same time I must
say that in my opinion your old striped Gown would have
been quite fine enough for its wearer—for to tell you the
truth (I always speak my mind) I am very much afraid
that one half of the people in the room will not know
whether you have a Gown on or not—But I suppose you
intend to make your fortune tonight—Well, the sooner
the better; & I wish you success."

"Indeed Ma'am I have no such intention.—"

"Who ever heard a Young Lady own that she was a
Fortune-hunter?" Miss Greville laughed, but I am sure
Ellen felt for me.

"Was your Mother gone to bed before you left her?"
said her Ladyship.

"Dear Ma'am" said Ellen, "it is but nine o'clock."

'True Ellen, but Candles cost money, and Mrs Williams is too wise to be extravagant."

"She was just sitting down to supper Ma'am."

"And what had she got for Supper?" "I did not observe." "Bread & Cheese I suppose." "I should never
wish for a better supper". said Ellen. "You have never
any reason" replied her Mother, "as a better is always
provided for you." Miss Greville laughed excessively, as
she constantly does at her Mother's wit.

Such is the humiliating Situation in which I am forced
to appear while riding in her Ladyship's Coach—I dare
not be impertinent, as my Mother is always admonishing
me to be humble & patient if I wish to make my way in
the world. She insists on my accepting every invitation
of Lady Greville, or you may be certain that I would
never enter either her House, or her Coach, with the disagreable certainty I always have of being abused for my
Poverty while I am in them.— When we arrived at Ash-
burnham, it was nearly ten o'clock, which was an hour
and a half later than we were desired to be there; but
Lady Greville is too fashionable (or fancies herself to be
so) to be punctual. The Dancing however was not begun
as they waited for Miss Greville. I had not been long in
the room before I was engaged to dance by Mr. Bernard
but just as we were going to stand up, he recollected that
his Servant had got his white Gloves, & immediately ran
out to fetch them. In the mean time the Dancing began
& Lady Greville in passing to another room went exactly
before me.— She saw me & instantly stopping, said to
me though there were several people close to us;

"Hey day, Miss Maria! What cannot you get a partner? Poor Young Lady! I am afraid your new Gown
was put on for nothing. But do not despair; perhaps you
may get a hop before the Evening is over." So saying,
she passed on without hearing my repeated assurance of
being engaged, & leaving me very provoked at being so
exposed before every one—Mr Bernard however soon
returned & by coming to me the moment he entered the
room, and leading me to the Dancers, my Character I
hope was cleared from the imputation Lady Greville had

thrown on it, in the eyes of all the old Ladies who had heard her speech. I soon forgot all my vexations in the pleasure of dancing and of having the most agreable partner in the room. As he is moreover heir to a very large Estate I could see that Lady Greville did not look very well pleased when she found who had been his Choice.— She was determined to mortify me, and accordingly when we were sitting down between the dances, she came to me with *more* than her usual insulting importance attended by Miss Mason and said loud enough to be heard by half the people in the room, "Pray Miss Maria in what way of business was your Grandfather? for Miss Mason & I cannot agree whether he was a Grocer or a Bookbinder." I saw that she wanted to mortify me and was resolved if I possibly could to prevent her seeing that her scheme succeeded. "Neither Madam; he was a Wine Merchant." "Aye, I knew he was in some such low way—He broke did not he?" "I beleive not Ma'am." "Did not he abscond?" "I never heard that he did" "At least he died insolvent?" "I was never told so before." "Why was not your Father as poor as a Rat?" "I fancy not;" "Was not he in the Kings Bench once?" "I never saw him there." *She* gave me *such* a look, & turned away in a great passion; while I was half delighted with myself for my impertinence, & half afraid of being thought too saucy. As Lady Greville was extremely angry with me, she took no further notice of me all the evening, and indeed had I been in favour I should have been equally neglected, as she was got into a party of great folks & she never speaks to me when she can to any one else. Miss Greville was with her Mother's party at Supper but Ellen preferred staying with the Bernards & me. We had a very pleasant Dance & as Lady G—slept all the way home, I had a very comfortable ride.

The next day while we were at dinner Lady Greville's Coach stopped at the door, for that is the time of day she generally contrives it should. She sent in a message

by the Servant to say that "she should not get out but
that Miss Maria must come to the Coach-door, as she
wanted to speak to her, and that she must make haste &
come immediately—" "What an impertinent Message
Mama!" said I— "Go Maria—" replied She—Accordingly I went & was obliged to stand there at her Lady-
ships pleasure though the Wind was extremely high and
very cold.

"Why I think Miss Maria you are not quite so smart
as you were last night—But I did not come to examine
your dress, but to tell you that you may dine with us the
day after tomorrow—Not tomorrow, remember, do not
come tomorrow, for we expect Lord and Lady Clermont
& Sir Thomas Stanley's family—There will be no occasion for your being very fine for I shant send the Carriage
—If it rains you may take an umbrella—" I could hardly
help laughing at hearing her give me leave to keep myself
dry—"and pray remember to be in time, for I shant
wait—I hate my Victuals over-done—But you need not
come *before* the time—How does your Mother do—? She
is at dinner is not she?" "Yes Ma'am we were in the
middle of dinner when your Ladyship came." "I am
afraid you find it very cold Maria." said Ellen. "Yes, it
is an horrible East wind"—said her Mother—"I assure
you I can hardly bear the window down—But you are
used to be blown about the wind Miss Maria & that is
what has made your Complexion so ruddy & coarse.
You young Ladies who cannot often ride in a Carriage
never mind what weather you trudge in, or how the
wind shews your legs. I would not have *my* Girls stand
out of doors as you do in such a day as this. But some sort
of people have no feelings either of cold or Delicacy—
Well, remember that we shall expect you on Thursday
at 5 o'clock—You must tell your Maid to come for you
at night—There will be no Moon—and you will have
an horrid walk home—My Compts to your Mother—I
am afraid your dinner will be cold—Drive on—" And

away she went, leaving me in a great passion with her as
she always does.

Maria Williams

Letter the fourth

From a young Lady rather impertinent to
her freind.

We dined yesterday with Mr Evelyn where we were introduced to a very agreable looking Girl his cousin. I
was extremely pleased with her appearance, for added to
the charms of an engaging face, her manner & voice had
something peculiarly interesting in them. So much so,
that they inspired me with a great curiosity to know the
history of her Life, who were her Parents, where she came
from, and what had befallen her, for it was then only
known that she was a relation of Mrs Evelyn, and that
her name was Grenville. In the evening a favourable
opportunity offered to me of attempting at least to know
what I wished to know, for every one played at Cards
but Mrs Evelyn, My Mother, Dr Drayton, Miss Grenville and myself, and as the two former were engaged in
a whispering Conversation, & the Doctor fell asleep, we
were of necessity obliged to entertain each other. This
was what I wished and being determined not to remain
in ignorance for want of asking, I began the Conversation
in the following Manner.

"Have you been long in Essex Ma'am?"

"I arrived on Tuesday".

"You came from Derbyshire?"

"No Ma'am!" appearing surprised at my question,
"from Suffolk." You will think this a good dash of mine
my dear Mary, but you will know that I am not wanting
for Impudence when I have any end in veiw." "Are you
pleased with the Country Miss Grenville? Do you find
it equal to the one you have left?"

"Much superior Ma'am in point of Beauty." She

sighed. I longed to know for why.

"But the face of any Country however beautiful" said I, "can be but a poor consolation for the loss of one's dearest Freinds." She shook her head, as if she felt the truth of what I said. My Curiosity was so much raised, that I was resolved at any rate to satisfy it.

"You regret having left Suffolk then Miss Grenville?" "Indeed I do." "You were born there I suppose?" "Yes Ma'am I was & passed many happy years there—".

"That is a great comfort—said I—I hope Ma'am that you never spent any *un*happy one's there."

"Perfect Felicity is not the property of Mortals, & no one has a right to expect uninterrupted Happiness— *Some* Misfortunes I have certainly met with—."

"*What* Misfortunes dear Ma'am?" replied I, burning with impatience to know every thing. "*None* Ma'am I hope that have been the effect of any wilfull fault in me." "I dare say not Ma'am, & have no doubt but that any sufferings you may have experienced could arise only from the cruelties of Relations or the Errors of Freinds." She sighed—"You seem unhappy my dear Miss Grenville —Is it in my power to soften your Misfortunes." "*Your* power Ma'am replied she extremely surprised; it is in *no ones* power to make me happy." She pronounced these words in so mournfull & solemn an accent, that for some time I had not courage to reply. I was actually silenced. I recovered myself however in a few moments & looking at her with all the affection I could, "My dear Miss Grenville said I, you appear extremely young—& may probably stand in need of some one's advice whose regard for you, joined to superior Age, perhaps superior Judgement might authorise her to give it—. I am that person, & I now challenge you to accept the offer I make you of my Confidence and Freindship, in return to which I shall only ask for yours—."

"You are extremely obliging Ma'am—said She—& I am highly flattered by your attention to me—. But I am in no difficulty, no doubt, no uncertainty of situation in which any Advice can be wanted. Whenever I am however continued she brightening into a complaisant smile, I shall know where to apply."

I bowed, but felt a good deal mortified by such a repulse; Still however I had not given up my point. I found that by the appearance of Sentiment & Freindship nothing was to be gained & determined therefore to renew my Attacks by Questions & Suppositions. "Do you intend staying long in this part of England Miss Grenville?"

"Yes Ma'am, some time I beleive."

"But how will Mr & Mrs Grenville bear your Absence?"

"They are neither of them alive Ma'am."

This was an answer I did not expect—I was quite silenced & never felt so awkward in my Life—.

Letter the fifth

From a Young Lady very much in love to her Freind.

My Uncle gets more stingy, my Aunt more particular, & I more in love every day. What shall we all be at this rate by the end of the year! I had this morning the happiness of receiving the following Letter from my dear Musgrove.

Sackville St: Jan:ry 7th

It is a month to day since I beheld my lovely Henrietta, & the sacred anniversary must & shall be kept in a manner becoming the day—by writing to her. Never shall I forget the moment when her Beauties first broke on my sight—No time as you well know can erase it from my Memory. It was at Lady Scudamores. Happy Lady Scudamore to live within a mile of the divine Henrietta! When the lovely Creature first entered the room, Oh!

what were my sensations? The sight of you was like the sight of a wonderful fine Thing. I started—I gazed at her with Admiration—She appeared every moment more Charming, and the unfortunate Musgrove became a Captive to your Charms before I had time to look about me. Yes Madam, I had the happiness of adoring you, an happiness for which I cannot be too grateful. "What said he to himself is Musgrove allowed to die for Henrietta? Enviable Mortal; and may he pine for her who is the object of universal Admiration, who is adored by a Colonel, & toasted by a Baronet! Adorable Henrietta how beautiful you are! I declare you are quite divine! You are more than Mortal. You are an angel. You are Venus herself. In short Madam you are the prettiest Girl I ever saw in my Life—& her beauty is encreased in her Musgroves Eyes, by permitting him to love her & allowing me to hope. And Ah! Angelic Miss Henrietta Heaven is my Witness how ardently I do hope for the death of your villanous Uncle & his Abandoned Wife, Since my fair one will not consent to be mine till their decease has placed her in affluence above what my fortune can procure—. Though it is an improvable Estate—. Cruel Henrietta to persist in such a resolution! I am at present with my Sister where I mean to continue till my own house which tho' an excellent one is at present somewhat out of repair, is ready to receive me. Amiable princess of my Heart farewell—Of that heart which trembles while it signs itself your most ardent Admirers & devoted humble Serv.t.

T. Musgrove

There is a pattern for a Love-letter Matilda! Did you ever read such a masterpeice of Writing? Such Sense, Such Sentiment, Such purity of Thought, Such flow of Language & such unfeigned Love in one Sheet? No, never I can answer for it, since a Musgrove is not to be met with by every Girl. Oh! how I long to be with him!

I intend to send him the following in answer to his Letter tomorrow.

My dearest Musgrove—. Words can not express how happy your Letter made me; I thought I should have cried for Joy, for I love you better than any body in the World. I think you the most amiable, & the handsomest Man in England, & so to be sure you are. I never read so sweet a Letter in my Life. Do write me another just like it, & tell me you are in love with me in every other line. I quite die to see you. How shall we manage to see one another? for we are so much in love that we cannot live asunder. Oh! my dear Musgrove you cannot think how impatiently I wait for the death of my Uncle and Aunt—If they will not die soon, I beleive I shall run mad, for I get more in love with you every day of my Life.

How happy your Sister is to enjoy the pleasure of your Company in her house, and how happy every body in London must be because you are there. I hope you will be so kind as to write to me again soon, for I never read such sweet Letters as yours. I am my dearest Musgrove most truly & faithfully yours for ever & ever. Henrietta Halton

I hope he will like my answer; it is as good a one as I can write, though nothing to his; Indeed I had always heard what a dab he was at a Love-letter. I saw him you know for the first time at Lady Scudamore's—And when I saw her Ladyship afterwards she asked me how I liked her Cousin Musgrove?

"Why upon my word said I, I think he is a very handsome young Man."

"I am glad you think so replied she, for he is distractedly in love with you."

"Law! Lady Scudamore, said I, how can you talk so ridiculously?"

"Nay, t'is very true answered She, I assure you, for he was in love with you from the first moment he beheld you."

"I wish it may be true said I, for that is the only kind of love I would give a farthing for—There is some Sense in being in love at first sight."

"Well, I give you Joy of your conquest, replied Lady Scudamore, and I beleive it to have been a very complete one; I am sure it is not a contemptible one, for my Cousin is a charming young fellow, has seen a great deal of the World, and writes the best Love-letters I ever read"

This made me very happy, and I was excessively pleased with my conquest. However, I thought it proper to give myself a few Airs—So I said to her—

"This is all very pretty Lady Scudamore, but you know that we young Ladies who are Heiresses must not throw ourselves away upon Men who have no fortune at all."

"My dear Miss Halton said She, I am as much convinced of that as you can be, and I do assure you that I should be the last person to encourage your marrying any one who had not some pretentions to expect a fortune with you. Mr Musgrove is so far from being poor that he has an estate of Several hundreds an year which is capable of great Improvement, and an excellent House, though at present it is not quite in repair."

"If that is the case replied I, I have nothing more to say against him, and if as you say he is an informed young Man and can write good Love-letters, I am sure I have no reason to find fault with him for admiring me, tho' perhaps I may not marry him for all that Lady Scudamore."

"You are certainly under no obligation to marry him answered her Ladyship, except that which love himself will dictate to you, for if I am not greatly mistaken you are at this very moment unknown to yourself, cherishing a most tender affection for him."

"Law, Lady Scudamore replied I blushing how can you think of such a thing?"

"Because every look, every word betrays it, answered

She; Come my dear Henrietta, consider me as a freind,
and be sincere with me—Do not you prefer Mr Musgrove to any man of your acquaintance?"

"Pray do not ask me such questions Lady Scudamore,
said I turning away my head, for it is not fit for me to
answer them."

"Nay my Love replied she, now you confirm my suspicions. But why Henrietta should you be ashamed to
own a well-placed Love, or why refuse to confide in me?"

"I am not ashamed to own it; said I taking Courage.
I do not refuse to confide in you or blush to say that I
do love your cousin Mr Musgrove, that I am sincerely
attached to him, for it is no disgrace to love a handsome
Man. If he were plain indeed I might have had reason to
be ashamed of a passion which must have been mean
since the Object would have been unworthy. But with
such a figure & face, & such beautiful hair as your
Cousin has, why should I blush to own that such Superior
Merit has made an impression on me."

"My sweet Girl (said Lady Scudamore embracing me
with great Affection) what a delicate way of thinking you
have in these Matters, and what a quick discernment for
one of your years! Oh! how I honour you for such Noble
Sentiments!"

"Do you Ma'am? said I; You are vastly obliging. But
pray Lady Scudamore did your Cousin himself tell you
of his Affection for me? I shall like him the better if he
did, for what is a Lover without a Confidante?"

"Oh! my Love replied She, you were born for each
other. Every word you say more deeply convinces me
that your Minds are actuated by the invisible power of
simpathy, for your opinions and Sentiments so exactly
coincide. Nay, the colour of your Hair is not very different. Yes my dear Girl, the poor despairing Musgrove
did reveal to me the story of his Love—. Nor was I surprised at it—I know not how it was, but I had a kind of
presentiment that he *would* be in love with you."

"Well, but how did he break it to you?"

"It was not till after supper. We were sitting round the fire together talking on indifferent subjects, though to say the truth the Conversation was cheifly on my side, for he was thoughtful and silent, when on a sudden he interrupted me in the midst of something I was saying, by exclaiming in a most Theatrical tone—

Yes I'm in love I feel it now

And Henrietta Halton has undone me—"

"Oh! What a Sweet Way replied I, of declaring his Passion! To make such a couple of charming Lines about me! What a pity it is that they are not in rhime!"

"I am very glad you like it, answered She; To be sure there was a great deal of Taste in it. And are you in love with her, Cousin? said I. I am very sorry for it, for unexceptionable as you are in every respect, with a pretty Estate capable of Great improvements, and an excellent House tho' somewhat out of repair, Yet who can hope to aspire with success to the adorable Henrietta who has had an offer from a Colonel & been toasted by a Baronet"—"*That* I have—" cried I. Lady Scudamore continued. "Ah dear Cousin replied he, I am so well convinced of the little Chance I can have of winning her who is adored by thousands, that I need no assurances of yours to make me more thoroughly so. Yet surely neither you or the fair Henrietta herself will deny me the exquisite Gratification of dieing for her, of falling a victim of her Charms. And when I am dead"—continued he—

"Oh Lady Scudamore," said I wiping my eyes, "that such a sweet Creature should talk of dieing!"

"It is an affecting Circumstance indeed," replied Lady Scudamore. "When I am dead said he, Let me be carried & lain at her feet, & perhaps she may not disdain to drop a pitying tear on my poor remains."

"Dear Lady Scudamore interrupted I, say no more on this affecting Subject. I cannot bear it."

"Oh! how I admire the sweet sensibility of your Soul, and as I would not for Worlds wound it too deeply, I will be silent."

"Pray go on" said I. She did so.

"And then added he, Ah! Cousin imagine what my transports will be when I feel the dear precious drops trickle on my face! Who would not die to taste such extacy! And when I am interred, may the divine Henrietta bless some happier Youth with her affection, May he be as tenderly attached to her as the hapless Musgrove & while *he* crumbles to dust, May they live an example of Felicity in the Conjugal state!"

Did you ever hear any thing so pathetic? What a charming wish, to be lain at my feet when he was dead! Oh! what an exalted mind he must have to be capable of such a wish! Lady Scudamore went on.

"Ah! my dear Cousin, replied I to him, such noble behaviour as this, must melt the heart of any Woman however obdurate it may naturally be; and could the divine Henrietta but hear your generous wishes for her happiness, all gentle as is her mind, I have not a doubt but that she would pity your affection & endeavour to return it." "Oh! Cousin answered he, do not endeavour to raise my hopes by such flattering Assurances. No, I cannot hope to please this angel of a Woman, and the only thing which remains for me to do, is to die." "True Love is ever desponding replied I, but *I* my dear Tom will give you even greater hopes of conquering this fair one's heart, than I have yet given you, by assuring you that I watched her with the strictest attention during the whole day, and could plainly discover that she cherishes in her bosom though unknown to herself, a most tender affection for you."

"Dear Lady Scudamore cried I, This is more than I ever knew!"

"Did I not say that it was unknown to yourself? I did not, continued I to him, encourage you by saying this at first, that Surprise might render the pleasure Still Greater." "No Cousin replied he in a languid voice, nothing will convince me that *I* can have touched the heart of Henrietta Halton, and if you are deceived yourself, do not attempt deceiving me." "In short my Love it was the work of some hours for me to persuade the poor despairing Youth that you had really a preference for him; but when at last he could no longer deny the force of my arguments, or discredit what I told him, his transports, his Raptures, his Extacies are beyond my power to describe."

"Oh! the dear Creature, cried I, how passionately he loves me! But dear Lady Scudamore did you tell him that I was totally dependant on my Uncle & Aunt?"

"Yes, I told him everything."

"And what did he say?"

"He exclaimed with virulence against Uncles & Aunts; Accused the Laws of England for allowing them to possess their Estates when wanted by their Nephews and Neices, and wished *he* were in the House of Commons, that he might reform the Legislature, & rectify all its abuses."

"Oh! the sweet Man! What a spirit he has!" said I.

"He could not flatter himself he added, that the adorable Henrietta would condescend for his sake to resign those Luxuries & that Splendor to which She had been used, and accept only in exchange the Comforts and Elegancies which his limitted Income could afford her, even supposing that his house were in Readiness to receive her. I told him that it could not be expected that she would; it would be doing her an injustice to suppose her capable of giving up the power she now possesses & so nobly uses of doing such extensive Good to the poorer part of her fellow Creatures, merely for the gratification of you and herself."

"To be sure said I, *I* am very Charitable every now and then. And what did Mr Musgrove say to this?"

"He replied that he was under a melancholy Necessity of owning the truth of what I said, and therefore if he should be the happy Creature destined to be the Husband of the Beautiful Henrietta he must bring himself to wait, however impatiently for the fortunate day, when she might be freed from the power of worthless Relations and able to bestow herself on him."

What a noble Creature he is! Oh! Matilda what a fortunate one *I am* who am to be his Wife! My Aunt is calling to me to come & make the pies, So adeiu my dear freind, & beleive me your &c.—H. Halton.

Finis

~~~~~~~~~~~~~~~~~~~~~~~~~~~~~~~~~~

THE
THREE
SISTERS

A NOVEL

~~~~~~~~~~~~~~~~~~~~~~~~~~~~~~~~~~

To Edward Austen Esqre
The following unfinished Novel
is respectfully inscribed
by
His obedient humle servt
THE AUTHOR

Letter 1st

MY DEAR FANNY

I am the happiest creature in the World, for I have received an offer of marriage from Mr Watts. It is the first I have ever had & I hardly know how to value it enough. How I will triumph over the Duttons! I do not intend to accept it, at least I beleive not, but as I am not quite certain I gave him an equivocal answer & left him. And now my dear Fanny I want your Advice whether I should accept his offer or not, but that you may be able to judge of his merits & the situation of affairs I will give you an account of them. He is quite an old Man, about two & thirty, very plain, *so* plain that I cannot bear to look at him. He is extremely disagreable & I hate him more than any body else in the world. He has a large fortune & will make great Settlements on me; but then he is very healthy. In short I do not know what to do. If I refuse him he as good as told me that he should offer himself to Sophia and if *she* refused him to Georgiana, & I could not bear to have either of them married before me. If I accept him I know I shall be miserable all the rest of my Life, for he is very ill tempered & peevish extremely jealous, & so stingy that there is no living in the house with him. He told me he should mention the affair to Mama, but I insisted upon it that he did not for very likely she would make me marry him whether I would or no; however probably he *has* before now, for he never does anything he is desired to do. I beleive I shall have him. It will be such a triumph to be married before Sophy, Georgiana & the Duttons; And he promised to have a new Carriage on the occasion, but we almost

quarrelled about the colour, for I insisted upon its being
blue spotted with silver, & he declared it should be a
plain Chocolate; & to provoke me more said it should
be just as low as his old one. I wont have him I declare.
He said he should come again tomorrow & take my final
answer, so I beleive I must get him while I can. I know
the Duttons will envy me & I shall be able to chaprone
Sophy & Georgiana to all the Winter Balls. But then
what will be the use of that when very likely he wont let
me go myself for I know he hates dancing & has a great
idea of Womens never going from home what he hates
himself he has no idea of any other person's liking; &
besides he talks a great deal of Women's always staying
at home & such stuff. I beleive I shant have him; I
would refuse him at once if I were certain that neither
of my Sisters would accept him, & that if they did not, he
would not offer to the Duttons. I cannot run such a risk,
so, if he will promise to have the Carriage ordered as I
like, I will have him, if not he may ride in it by himself
for me. I hope you like my determination; I can think
of nothing better;

   And am your ever Affecte

                                   MARY STANHOPE

FROM THE SAME TO THE SAME

DEAR FANNY

I had but just sealed my last letter to you when my
Mother came up & told me she wanted to speak to me
on a very particular subject.

   "Ah! I know what you mean; (said I) That old fool
Mr Watts has told you all about it, tho' I bid him not.
However you shant force me to have him if I don't like
it."

   "I am not going to force you Child, but only want to
know what your resolution is with regard to his Proposals,
& to insist upon your making up your mind one way or
t'other, that if *you* dont accept him *Sophy* may."

"Indeed (replied I hastily) Sophy need not trouble herself for I shall certainly marry him myself."

"If that is your resolution" (said my Mother) why should you be afraid of my forcing your inclinations?"

"Why, because I have not settled whether I shall have him or not."

"You are the strangest Girl in the World Mary. What you say one moment, you unsay the next. Do tell me once for all, whether you intend to marry Mr Watts or not?"

"Law Mama how can I tell you what I dont know myself?"

"Then I desire you will know, & quickly too, for Mr Watts says he wont be kept in suspense."

"That depends upon me."

"No it does not, for if you do not give him your final answer tomorrow when he drinks Tea with us, he intends to pay his Addresses to Sophy."

"Then I shall tell all the World that he behaved very ill to me."

"What good will that do? Mr Watts has been too long abused by all the World to mind it now."

"I wish I had a Father or a Brother because then they should fight him."

"They would be cunning if they did, for Mr Watts would run away first; & therefore you must & shall resolve either to accept or refuse him before tomorrow evening."

"But why if I don't have him, must he offer to my Sisters?"

"Why! because he wishes to be allied to the Family & because they are as pretty as you are."

"But will Sophy marry him Mama if he offers to her?"

"Most likely, Why should not she? If however she does not choose it, then Georgiana must, for I am determined not to let such an opportunity escape of settling one of my Daughters so advantageously. So, make the most of

your time; I leave you to settle the Matter with yourself." And then she went away. The only thing I can
think of my dear Fanny is to ask Sophy & Georgiana
whether they would have him were he to make proposals
to them, & if they say they would not I am resolved to
refuse him too, for I hate him more than you can imagine.
As for the Duttons if he marries one of *them* I shall still
have the triumph of having refused him first. So, adeiu
my dear Freind—

Yrs ever M.S.

MISS GEORGIANA STANHOPE TO MISS XXX

Wednesday

MY DEAR ANNE

Sophy & I have just been practising a little deceit on our
eldest Sister, to which we are not perfectly reconciled,
& yet the circumstances were such that if any thing will
excuse it, they must. Our neighbour Mr Watts has made
proposals to Mary: Proposals which she knew not how
to receive for tho' she has a particular Dislike to him (in
which she is not singular) yet she would willingly marry
him sooner than risk his offering to Sophy or me which
in case of a refusal from herself, he told her he should do,
for you must know the poor Girl considers our marrying
before her as one of the greatest misfortunes that can
possibly befall her, & to prevent it would willingly ensure herself everlasting Misery by a Marriage with Mr
Watts. An hour ago she came to us to sound our inclinations respecting the affair which were to determine
hers. A little before she came my Mother had given us
an account of it, telling us that she certainly would not
let him go farther than our own family for a Wife. "And
therefore (said she) If Mary won't have him Sophy must,
& if Sophy wont Georgiana *shall*". Poor Georgiana!—
We neither of us attempted to alter my Mother's resolution, which I am sorry to say is generally more strictly

kept than rationally formed. As soon as she was gone
however I broke silence to assure Sophy that if Mary
should refuse Mr Watts I should not expect her to sacri-
fice *her* happiness by becoming his Wife from a motive of
Generosity to me, which I was afraid her Good nature
& sisterly affection might induce her to do.

"Let us flatter ourselves (replied She) that Mary will
not refuse him. Yet how can I hope that my Sister may
accept a Man who cannot make her happy."

"*He* cannot it is true but his Fortune, his Name, his
House, his Carriage will and I have no doubt but that
Mary will marry him; indeed why should she not? He is
not more than two & thirty; a very proper age for a
Man to marry at; He is rather plain to be sure, but then
what is Beauty in a Man; if he has but a genteel figure
& a sensible looking Face it is quite sufficient."

"This is all very true Georgiana but Mr Watts's figure
is unfortunately extremely vulgar & his Countenance is
very heavy."

"And then as to his temper; it has been reckoned bad,
but may not the World be deceived in their Judgement
of it. There is an open Frankness in his Disposition which
becomes a Man; They say he is stingy; We'll call that
Prudence. They say he is suspicious. *That* proceeds from
a warmth of Heart always excusable in Youth, & in
short I see no reason why he should not make a very
good Husband, or why Mary should not be very happy
with him."

Sophy laughed; I continued,

"However whether Mary accepts him or not I am resolved. My determination is made. I never would marry
Mr Watts were Beggary the only alternative. So deficient
in every respect! Hideous in his person and without one
good Quality to make amends for it. His fortune to be
sure is good. Yet not so very large! Three thousand a year.
What is three thousand a year? It is but six times as
much as my Mother's income. It will not tempt me."

"Yet it will be a noble fortune for Mary" said Sophy laughing again.

"For Mary! Yes indeed it will give me pleasure to see *her* in such affluence."

Thus I ran on to the great Entertainment of my Sister till Mary came into the room to appearance in great agitation. She sate down. We made room for her at the fire. She seemed at a loss how to begin & at last said in some confusion

"Pray Sophy have you any mind to be married?"

"To be married! None in the least. But why do you ask me? Are you acquainted with any one who means to make me proposals?"

"I—no, how should I? But mayn't I ask a common question?"

"Not a very *common* one Mary surely." (said I). She paused & after some moments silence went on—

"How should you like to marry Mr Watts Sophy?"

I winked at Sophy & replied for her. "Who is there but must rejoice to marry a man of three thousand a year who keeps a postchaise & pair, with silver Harness, a boot before & a window to look out at behind?"

"Very true (she replied) That's very true. So you would have him if he would offer, Georgiana, & would *you* Sophy?"

Sophy did not like the idea of telling a lie & deceiving her Sister; she prevented the first & saved half her conscience by equivocation.

"I should certainly act just as Georgiana would do."

"Well then said Mary with triumph in her Eyes, *I* have had an offer from Mr Watts."

We were of course very much surprised; "Oh! do not accept him said I, and then perhaps he may have me."

In short my scheme took & Mary is resolved to do *that* to prevent our supposed happiness which she would not have done to ensure it in reality. Yet after all my Heart cannot acquit me & Sophy is even more scrupulous.

Quiet our Minds my dear Anne by writing & telling us you approve our conduct. Consider it well over. Mary will have real pleasure in being a married Woman, & able to chaprone us, which she certainly shall do, for I think myself bound to contribute as much as possible to her happiness in a State I have made her choose. They will probably have a new Carriage, which will be paradise to her, & if we can prevail on Mr. W. to set up his Phaeton she will be too happy. These things however would be no consolation to Sophy or me for domestic Misery. Remember all this & do not condemn us.

Friday

Last night Mr Watts by appointment drank tea with us. As soon as his Carriage stopped at the Door, Mary went to the Window.

"Would you beleive it Sophy (said she) the old Fool wants to have his new Chaise just the colour of the old one, & hung as low too. But it shant—I *will* carry my point. And if he wont let it be as high as the Duttons, & blue spotted with silver, I won't have him. Yes I will too. Here he comes. I know he'll be rude; I know he'll be illtempered & wont say one civil thing to me! nor behave at all like a Lover." She then sate down & Mr Watts entered.

"Ladies your most obedient." We paid our Compliments & he seated himself.

"Fine weather Ladies." Then turning to Mary, "Well Miss Stanhope I hope you have *at last* settled the Matter in your own mind; & will be so good as to let me know whether you will *condescend* to marry me or not".

"I think Sir (said Mary) You might have asked in a genteeler way than that. I do not know whether I *shall* have you if you behave so odd."

"Mary!" (said my Mother) "Well Mama if he will be so cross. . . . ."

"Hush, hush, Mary, you shall not be rude to Mr Watts."

"Pray Madam do not lay any restraint on Miss Stanhope by obliging her to be civil. If she does not choose to accept my hand, I can offer it else where, for as I am by no means guided by a particular preference to you above your Sisters it is equally the same to me which I marry of the three." Was there ever such a Wretch! Sophy reddened with anger, & I felt *so* spiteful!

"Well then (said Mary in a peevish Accent) I *will* have you if I *must*."

"I should have thought Miss Stanhope that when such Settlements are offered as I have offered to you there can be no great violence done to the inclinations in accepting of them."

Marry mumbled out something, which I who sate close to her could just distinguish to be "What's the use of a great Jointure if Men live forever?" And then audibly "Remember the pinmoney; two hundred a year."

"A hundred and seventy-five Madam."

"Two hundred indeed Sir" said my Mother.

"And Remember I am to have a new Carriage hung as high as the Duttons', & blue spotted with silver; and I shall expect a new saddle horse, a suit of fine lace, and an infinite number of the most valuable Jewels. Diamonds such as never were seen, and Pearls, Rubies, Emeralds and Beads out of number. You must set up your Phaeton which must be cream coloured with a wreath of silver flowers round it, You must buy 4 of the finest Bays in the Kingdom & you must drive me in it every day. This is not all; You must entirely new furnish your House after my Taste, You must hire two more Footmen to attend me, two Women to wait on me, must always let me do just as I please & make a very good husband."

Here she stopped, I beleive rather out of breath.

"This is all very reasonable Mr Watts for my Daughter to expect."

"And it is very reasonable Mrs Shanhope that your daughter should be disappointed." He was going on but Mary interupted him "You must build me an elegant Greenhouse & stock it with plants. You must let me spend every Winter in Bath, every Spring in Town, Every Summer in taking some Tour, & every Autumn at a Watering Place, and if we are at home the rest of the year (Sophy & I laughed) You must do nothing but give Balls & Masquerades. You must build a room on purpose & a Theatre to act Plays in. The first Play we have shall be *Which is the Man*, and I will do Lady Bell Bloomer."

"And pray Miss Stanhope (said Mr Watts) What am I to expect from you in return for all this."

"Expect? why you may expect to have me pleased."

"It would be odd if I did not. Your expectations Madam are too high for me, & I must apply to Miss Sophy who perhaps may not have raised her's so much."

"You are mistaken Sir in supposing so, (said Sophy) for tho' they may not be exactly in the same Line, yet my expectations are to the full as high as my Sister's; for I expect my Husband to be good tempered & Chearful; to consult my Happiness in all his Actions, & to love me with Constancy & Sincerity."

Mr Watts stared. "There are very odd Ideas truly young Lady. You had better discard them before you marry, or you will be obliged to do it afterwards."

My Mother in the meantime was lecturing Mary who was sensible that she had gone too far, & when Mr Watts was just turning towards me in order I beleive to address me, she spoke to him in a voice half humble, half sulky.

"You are mistaken Mr Watts if you think I was in earnest when I said I expected so much. However I must have a new Chaise."

"Yes Sir, you must allow that Mary has a right to expect that."

"Mrs Stanhope, I *mean* & have always meant to have

a new one on my Marriage. But it shall be the colour of
my present one."

"I think Mr Watts you should pay my Girl the compli-
ment of consulting her Taste on such Matters."

Mr Watts would not agree to this, & for some time
insisted upon its being a Chocolate colour, while Mary
was as eager for having it blue with silver Spots. At
length however Sophy proposed that to please Mr W. it
should be a dark brown & to please Mary it should be
hung rather high & have a silver Border. This was at
length agreed to, tho' reluctantly on both sides, as each
had intended to carry their point entire. We then proceeded to other Matters, & it was settled that they should
be married as soon as the Writings could be completed.
Mary was very eager for a Special Licence & Mr Watts
talked of Banns. A common Licence was at last agreed
on. Mary is to have all the Family Jewels which are very
inconsiderable I beleive & Mr W. promised to buy her a
Saddle horse; but in return she is not to expect to go to
Town or any other public place for these three Years.
She is to have neither Greenhouse, Theatre or Phaeton;
to be contented with one Maid without an additional
Footman. It engrossed the whole Evening to settle these
affairs; Mr W. supped with us & did not go till twelve.
As soon as he was gone Mary exclaimed "Thank Heaven!
he's off at last; how I do hate him!" It was in vain that
Mama represented to her the impropriety she was guilty
of in disliking him who was to be her Husband, for she
persisted in declaring her aversion to him & hoping she
might never see him again. What a Wedding will this
be! Adeiu my dear Anne. Yr faithfully Sincere

GEORGIANA STANHOPE

FROM THE SAME TO THE SAME
Saturday

DEAR ANNE
Mary eager to have every one know of her approaching

Wedding & more particularly desirous of triumphing as
she called it over the Duttons, desired us to walk with
her this Morning to Stoneham. As we had nothing else
to do we readily agreed, & had as pleasant a walk as we
could have with Mary whose conversation entirely consisted in abusing the Man she is so soon to marry & in
longing for a blue Chaise spotted with Silver. When we
reached the Duttons we found the two Girls in the dressing-room with a very handsome Young Man, who was
of course introduced to us. He is the son of Sir Henry
Brudenell of Leicestershire—. Mr Brudenell is the handsomest Man I ever saw in my Life; we are all three very
much pleased with him. Mary, who from the moment of
our reaching the Dressing-room had been swelling with
the knowledge of her own importance & with the Desire
of making it known, could not remain long silent on the
Subject after we were seated, & soon addressing herself
to Kitty said,

"Dont you think it will be necessary to have all the
Jewels new set?"

"Necessary for what?"

"For What! Why for my appearance."

"I beg your pardon but I really do not understand
you. What Jewels do you speak of, & where is your appearance to be made?"

"At the next Ball to be sure after I am married."

You may imagine their Surprise. They were at first
incredulous, but on our joining in the Story they at last
beleived it. "And who is it to" was of course the first
Question. Mary pretended Bashfulness, & answered in
Confusion her Eyes cast down "to Mr Watts". This also
required Confirmation from us, for that anyone who had
the Beauty & fortune (tho' small yet a provision) of Mary
would willingly marry Mr Watts, could by them scarcely
be credited. The subject being now fairly introduced and
she found herself the object of every one's attention in
company, she lost all her confusion & became perfectly

unreserved & communicative.

"I wonder you should never have heard of it before for in general things of this Nature are very well known in the Neighbourhood."

"I assure you said Jemina I never had the least suspicion of such an affair. Has it been in agitation long?"

"Oh! Yes, ever since Wednesday."

They all smiled particularly Mr Brudenell.

"You must know Mr Watts is very much in love with me, so that it is quite a match of affection on his side."

"Not on his only, I suppose" said Kitty.

"Oh! when there is so much Love on one side there is no occasion for it on the other. However I do not much dislike him tho' he is very plain to be sure."

Mr Brudenell stared, the Miss Duttons laughed & Sophy & I were heartily ashamed of our Sister. She went on.

"We are to have a new Postchaise & very likely may set up our Phaeton."

This we knew to be false but the poor Girl was pleased at the idea of persuading the company that such a thing was to be & I would not deprive her of so harmless an Enjoyment. She continued.

"Mr Watts is to present me with the family Jewels which I fancy are very considerable." I could not help whispering Sophy "I fancy not". "These Jewels are what I suppose must be new set before they can be worn. I shall not wear them till the first Ball I go to after my Marriage. If Mrs Dutton should not go to it, I hope you will let me chaprone you; I shall certainly take Sophy & Georgiana."

"You are very good (said Kitty) & since you are inclined to undertake the Care of young Ladies, I should advise you to prevail on Mrs Edgecumbe to let you chaprone her six Daughters which with your two Sisters and ourselves will make your Entrée very respectable."

Kitty made us all smile except Mary who did not understand her Meaning & coolly said that she should not like to chaprone so many. Sophy & I now endeavoured to change the conversation but succeeded only for a few Minutes, for Mary took care to bring back their attention to her & her approaching Wedding. I was sorry for my Sister's sake to see that Mr Brudenell seemed to take pleasure in listening to her account of it, & even encouraged her by his Questions & Remarks, for it was evident that his only Aim was to laugh at her. I am afraid he found her very ridiculous. He kept his Countenance extremely well, yet it was easy to see that it was with difficulty he kept it. At length however he seemed fatigued & Disgusted with her ridiculous Conversation, as he turned from her to us, & spoke but little to her fo about half an hour before we left Stoneham. As soon as we were out of the House we all joined in praising the Person & Manners of Mr Brudenell.

We found Mr Watts at home.

"So, Miss Stanhope (said he) you see I am come a courting in a true Lover like Manner."

"Well you need not have *told* me that. I knew why you came very well."

Sophy & I then left the room, imagining of course that we must be in the way, if a Scene of Courtship were to begin. We were surprised at being followed almost immediately by Mary.

"And is your Courting so soon over?" said Sophy.

"Courting! (replied Marry) we have been quarrelling. Watts is such a Fool! I hope I shall never see him again."

"I am afraid you will, (said I) as he dines here today. But what has been your dispute?"

"Why only because I told him that I had seen a Man much handsomer than he was this Morning, he flew into a great Passion & called me a Vixen, so I only stayed to tell him I thought him a Blackguard & came away."

"Short & sweet; (said Sophy) but pray Mary how will this be made up?"

"He ought to ask my pardon; but if he did, I would not forgive him."

"His Submission then would not be very useful."

When we were dressed we returned to the Parlour where Mama & Mr Watts were in close Conversation. It seems that he had been complaining to her of her Daughter's behaviour, & she had persuaded him to think no more of it. He therefore met Mary with all his accustomed Civility, & except one touch at the Phaeton & another at the Greenhouse, the Evening went off with great Harmony & Cordiality. Watts is going to Town to hasten the preparations for the Wedding.

                    I am your affecte Freind G.S.

                    Finis